BREAK IN, BLACK OUT

Gun in hand, Longarm edged on tiptoe across the floor to the doorway and felt for the doorknob. There was no quiet or easy way to do this. If Jimmy Jay wasn't in the front room, it wouldn't matter what he did anyway, so he might as well assume the worst.

Longarm braced himself, then jerked the bedroom door open and let out an earsplitting howl as he leaped through with the Colt leveled.

"Jesus God!" the man seated in the armchair cried out in alarm and dropped the Bible he'd been reading.

"Oh, damn," Longarm responded "I . . . there's been a mistake. I'm sorry, but I . . ."

He heard a faint thump behind him.

Then he heard a mighty thump. Inside his head.

Something very solid and very heavy smashed down onto the back of his head, and Longarm felt himself begin to fall.

He was no longer conscious when he ended that fall on the floor of the apartment he'd just broken into . . .

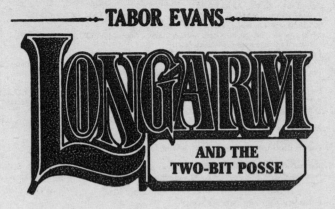

TABOR EVANS

LONGARM

AND THE TWO-BIT POSSE

JOVE BOOKS, NEW YORK

THE BERKLEY PUBLISHING GROUP
Published by the Penguin Group
Penguin Group (USA) Inc.
375 Hudson Street, New York, New York 10014, USA
Penguin Group (Canada), 10 Alcorn Avenue, Toronto, Ontario M4V 3B2, Canada
(a division of Pearson Penguin Canada Inc.)
Penguin Books Ltd., 80 Strand, London WC2R 0RL, England
Penguin Group Ireland, 25 St. Stephen's Green, Dublin 2, Ireland (a division of Penguin Books Ltd.)
Penguin Group (Australia), 250 Camberwell Road, Camberwell, Victoria 3124, Australia
(a division of Pearson Australia Group Pty. Ltd.)
Penguin Books India Pvt. Ltd., 11 Community Centre, Panchsheel Park, New Delhi—110 017, India
Penguin Group (NZ), Cnr. Airborne and Rosedale Roads, Albany, Auckland 1310, New Zealand
(a division of Pearson New Zealand Ltd.)
Penguin Books (South Africa) (Pty.) Ltd., 24 Sturdee Avenue, Rosebank, Johannesburg 2196, South
Africa

Penguin Books Ltd., Registered Offices: 80 Strand, London WC2R 0RL, England

This is a work of fiction. Names, characters, places, and incidents either are the product of the author's imagination or are used fictitiously, and any resemblance to actual persons, living or dead, business establishments, events, or locales is entirely coincidental.

LONGARM AND THE TWO-BIT POSSE

A Jove Book / published by arrangement with the author

PRINTING HISTORY
Jove edition / November 2004

Copyright © 2004 by The Berkley Publishing Group.

ISBN: 0-515-13853-3

JOVE®
Jove Books are published by The Berkley Publishing Group,
a division of Penguin Group (USA) Inc.
375 Hudson Street, New York, New York 10014.
JOVE is a registered trademark of Penguin Group (USA) Inc.
The "J" design is a trademark belonging to Penguin Group (USA) Inc.

PRINTED IN THE UNITED STATES OF AMERICA

10 9 8 7 6 5 4 3 2 1

Chapter 1

The girl had a body that would make Venus de Milo look like a hag. And this girl had arms. She used them to wrap herself around Custis Long's lean and very ready body.

She kissed him like she wanted to suck his tongue clean out of his mouth, and she clung to him with one leg in addition to both arms.

"You are so handsome," she whispered. "So strong." Her hands fondled the bulge in his trousers, and her eyes went wide. "Oh, my."

Longarm kissed her back, then released her so he could shuck his coat and gunbelt. Her name was Cherie, and they were in her room at the Bradford Hotel. They met when Cherie dropped her handbag, scattering its contents on the sidewalk in front of the Halliday Café on Grant.

He helped her retrieve her things, and her thanks led to coffee. Coffee led to lunch. And lunch led to the third floor of the Bradford.

Now Cherie was bare-assed and breathless.

She was one of those women—very rare women—who looked better naked than when they were dolled up in their prettiest clothing. She was a pale, petite little four foot, ten inch blonde with a waist that could probably be encircled by his spur straps, an ass that provided two cute handfuls . . . and tits the size of watermelons.

Cherie presented quite a contrast to Longarm, who stood well over six feet in height with broad shoulders, narrow hips, and a craggy face that was weathered brown by sun and wind. He had brown hair, brown eyes, and a luxuriant growth of mustache that got in the way not at all when Cherie probed his tonsils with the tip of her warm and very active tongue.

"You are such a lovely man," she said. Longarm thought there was a touch of sadness in her voice. Regret, he thought, although he could not imagine for what.

Cherie sighed.

And screamed.

Squeaked was really more like it. As screams went this one was pretty weak.

It was, however, loud enough to signal the man who was waiting behind the door that led into a connecting room.

The fellow looked like a gambler, albeit a rumpled and seedy one. His collar was limp and his cuffs frayed and whatever stone used to be in his stickpin was gone now, either lost or pried out and sold.

He was holding a small-bore pepperbox pistol. Probably a .31 caliber, Longarm judged with professional interest. The gun was aimed at Longarm's chest. A .31 in that spot, or even a .28, could ruin a fellow's whole day.

Cherie gave him an apologetic shrug and stepped clear of the line of fire. She positioned herself between Longarm and his own .44 Colt that lay now on a bedside chair. She seemed to know what she was doing.

"Sorry, dear," she said. "But you know how it goes."

"You might at least have given me a quickie first," Longarm said.

"I would have, dearie, but Frankie doesn't like to share his toys."

2

"Will you two please shut up," the skinny gambler snapped. "Mister, you prob'ly know how this is gonna work. You pay me a little something, a modest amount really, and there's no trouble. You go one way. We go another. Nobody gets hurt. Otherwise . . ." Frankie shrugged. "Cherie makes a complaint with this constable friend of hers on the city police force. He takes you to jail. You might be there for days before you could get a lawyer to get you out. What with fines and court costs and lawyer fees and all that, it could cost you three, four hundred dollars and a whole lot of embarrassment. They'd put your name in the newspapers and everything. All your friends and neighbors would know you accosted this poor young woman. Tried to force yourself on her. And wouldn't all of us hate for your neighbors to think you are that sort of person."

"But if I cooperate?" Longarm asked, his attention on Cherie, who was getting dressed again. My but she really was a good-looking girl. Sleek.

"We aren't greedy," Frankie said. "Let's figure it would cost you at the very least two hundred if the little lady has to press charges. Or you can pay us half that to make the whole thing go away. Now that sounds fair enough, doesn't it?"

"A hundred dollars," Longarm said.

"Yes, and a bargain at the price," Frankie told him. "Plus, don't forget, no one else has to know about it. No embarrassment before your business colleagues. No newspaper publicity." He smiled. "So you see we are saving you a great deal more than just the hundred dollars. We'll be saving your reputation, as well."

Longarm scratched the side of his nose. "You seem to have me by the short hairs, don't you?"

"Yes, that would be the general idea."

"Hand me my coat, would you please, Cherie?"

3

"Uh-uh. Careful," Frankie warned. "You don't know what could be in those pockets."

"My wallet is there," Longarm said. "You do want me to open my wallet, don't you?"

"All right, Cherie. Find the man's wallet and hand it to him. But just his wallet, not the whole coat."

"It's in the inside breast pocket," Longarm said.

The girl was fully dressed now. Darn it. Longarm looked at Frankie. "Do I at least get to fuck the girl at that price?"

"No, but I might let you do her for another hundred."

"Frankie!" Cherie squealed. "No."

"Believe me, mister, she's worth a hundred bucks. She might not be big, but once she gets that little ass moving it's like she's been hooked up to one of those mill wheels. She just goes and goes. Drain the sap right out of you, she can."

"I believe you," Longarm said, eyeing the girl up and down.

"Do you want to go the extra hundred for the little lady then, mister?"

"For all night?" Longarm asked. "A hundred is an awful lot of money for a piece of ass."

"But worth every penny, I promise you."

"Frankie, please. You already promised I wouldn't have to fuck anybody."

"Shut up, baby, and give the gentleman his wallet."

Cherie was pouting, but she did what she was told. She handed the wallet to Longarm and returned his coat to the back of the chair.

Longarm dipped the fingers of his right hand into his vest pocket. They emerged holding a brass-framed .41 caliber derringer that was aimed unerringly at Frankie's heart. With his left hand Longarm flipped his wallet open, exposing the nickeled pewter badge of a United States deputy marshal.

4

"I think I'd like to renegotiate the deal," he told Frankie.

"Oh, shit," Cherie moaned.

Frankie said nothing at all. But he did turn awfully pale.

Chapter 2

"Custis Long, deputy United States marshal," he introduced himself. "My friends call me Longarm. You can call me 'sir.' You can also toss that pepperbox onto the bed there. Cherie, I saw that little pig-sticker you slipped into your garter. Please put it on the bed with Frankie's pistol. There." He smiled. "Thank you. Both of you. Frankie, take your coat off for me, please. Oh, my. What do we have here? One of those cute little spring-loaded sleeve gadgets. Just the thing for drawing just exactly the card you need." Longarm shook his head in mock sadness. "Frankie, Frankie," he chided. "I am beginning to think that you are not honest."

"Look, uh, sir, why don't we come to an accommodation here. You can have the girl. For as long as you want her. She'll do anything you want. Anything. Really. And she really is as good as I told you. You can have her. No charge, of course, between friends. What do you say to that, huh?"

"Normally," Longarm lied, "I would consider taking you up on that generous offer, Frankie, but I have a quota to meet. Got to make so many arrests each month, you know, and this month I just happen t' be two felons short of making my minimum. Or was. 'Til now. You an' the little lady here put me right over the top. My boss is gonna be real happy with me, once I book you two in."

He pretended to ponder while he strapped his gunbelt back on, the big double-action Colt rigged to the left of the belt buckle for a cross-draw. "Let me see what I have on you two friendly folks. Let's start out with assault on a federal officer. That's five to ten years right there. Say you serve the minimum. Out in five years. That won't be so bad. Turn around, Frankie. Thank you."

Longarm peered at the scrawny gambler's back. "You got kind of a small ass on you, Frankie. But don't you worry none. Those boys in the jug will loosen it right up for you. An' you, Cherie, you won't be lonely, either, pretty little thing like you. Bat your eyelashes at the judge real nice, and you might not draw more than three years. You can do that easy enough."

Frankie was beginning to sweat. He turned around and pleaded, "Marshal Long . . . sir . . . we don't have anything to give you. Please. Can't we work something out here? Please?"

Longarm's expression hardened and turned serious. "Listen to me, you miserable little piece of shit, I wouldn't care if you had ten thousand dollars to lay down in cash right there on that bed, I wouldn't be interested. Not the least bit I wouldn't. I despise scum like you. Both of you." The girl winced and dropped her eyes.

"You prey on men who aren't doing anything but accepting something that's been offered to them. Then you shame and rob them. I don't know how many charges I can lay on you. Extortion. That one for sure, along with the assault."

"But I didn't . . ."

"Shut the fuck up. Yes, you did. Pointing that gun at me was an assault, the way the law looks at it. I got you cold on that one. Got the both of you for extortion. I'll put my head together with the prosecutors and see what else we can come up with. Maybe put you in the Colorado prison system for a few years, then send you over to Kansas to serve out the federal sentence. You could be inside eight, ten years, Frankie. Could be longer."

"I'm sick. I can't . . ."

"Then die in there. I really don't care. Or do you want to see if you can grab up that gun again? End everything right here with a bullet in your brain. Would you rather do that?"

"Please, no, Marshal," the girl begged. "Don't do that to him. I'll . . . Frankie was right, sweetie. I'll do whatever you want. For as long as you want. You want me to show you? You want me to start right now? I'll do it. Honest, I will."

"He means that much to you?"

Cherie began to cry. She nodded. "He does, Marshal. God help me, he really does."

"Then I feel sorry for you. But the fact remains. He'll be going to prison for a long time. If it makes you feel any better, you'll probably get off with just jail time. Maybe a year. You won't be in the federal prison system. Might even stay right here in the county. It won't be that bad. You'll see."

"But I could make you feel . . ."

"Hush, girl. Be quiet now before I have to charge you with attempted bribery of a federal officer. That would mean serving serious time."

"Mister . . . Marshal . . . could we maybe work out a trade?" she begged.

"I already told you . . ."

"No, no. I don't mean pussy. I mean how's about if we told you where you could find Leo Batson."

"Who is Leo Batson an' why would I want to bother finding him?" Longarm asked.

"You didn't know? Oh, dear. I suppose you don't," the

9

girl said. "Leo is the gentleman who has been blowing up all those mail pouches."

"This Batson guy is the Mail Bomber?"

"Yes, exactly."

"And you can tell me how to take him down?"

"I think so. Yes."

"We can, Marshal, sir. She's right. We could do that."

Longarm tugged at the left tip of his mustache and unconsciously twirled it into a tighter point. "I think . . . if you can prove up on this claim about the Mail Bomber . . . then we just might be able to work out something that would keep you out of prison," he said tentatively.

"Both of us?" the girl persisted.

"That would be up to the prosecutor and maybe a judge. It wouldn't be my call alone."

"But do you think they would go for it?"

"For the Mail Bomber . . . yes, I'm sure they would go for it."

Cherie looked at Frankie and lifted a prettily curved eyebrow. The gambler nodded.

Cherie sighed. "Poor Leo."

"Better him than us, baby."

"I know. You are right, dear. But Leo is such a nice man." She looked at Longarm and brightened. "It's a deal, then."

"Whoa," he said. "There are formalities that have to be gone through first."

"I have confidence in you, sweetie," Cherie said, coming close and reaching up to stroke Longarm's cheek. Then she reached down and stroked something else, which had settled down and gone soft again over the past couple of minutes.

Longarm checked his pockets before he stepped away from her, making sure the damn girl hadn't boosted his wallet or his derringer or something. Cherie, he judged, was not an entirely trustworthy young lady.

"Let's go see if we can find someone in the prosecutor's office to discuss this with," he suggested. "I won't bother to handcuff you. I know you are both dependable and good for your word. I also know I will shoot either or both of you square in the back if you try to run."

Frankie began to look pale again. The girl gave him a close, searching look, but found nothing there to suggest that Longarm would not do exactly what he said.

"You first, Frankie. We're going to the Federal Building. You know where that is?"

The gambler shook his head.

"Colfax Avenue," Longarm told him. "Right next door to the Denver Mint. And I'm sure you'll know where they make the money."

"I know the mint," Frankie conceded.

"Then lead the way, please, and if I seem to lag behind, don't you fret yourself over it. Col. Colt won't let me get too far away. You might want to keep that in mind."

Longarm took the girl by the elbow and urged them toward the hotel room door.

He wondered if they really did know how he could find the Mail Bomber. If this Leo fellow really was him. Jesus, until right this minute none of them had so much as a name for the son of a bitch. This could be a real breakthrough, if Cherie and Frankie were being straight with him about it. A real breakthrough.

Chapter 3

"Who the hell is Leo Batson?" Billy Vail asked. Vail was the United States marshal for the Justice Department's Denver district. Unlike most political appointees, Billy Vail was very good at the job of being a lawman. That did not make him very popular with the other political appointees, but it certainly gained him the respect of his deputies and of the prosecutors who worked with him.

Unlike Longarm, who looked the part of a peace officer, Billy Vail had the outward appearance of a storekeeper. He was balding and pink-cheeked and in recent years had begun to need reading glasses for close-up work. But before he became a U.S. marshal he was a Texas ranger, and a good many Texas felons learned not to cross him. The ones who failed that lesson tended to wind up dead. Longarm not only respected Billy Vail, he liked his boss, too.

Longarm crossed his legs and reached inside his coat for a cheroot. He and Billy were seated inside the marshal's office. Cherie and Frankie were in the outer office, waiting under the watchful eye of Billy's office manager, secretary, assistant, and sometime fill-in deputy, Henry.

"Don't light that," Billy said. "They stink the place up. Takes me hours to get the smell out."

"Be all right if I chew it?"

"You can put salt and pepper on and eat it right down if you like," Billy said. "Just don't light it."

Longarm stuck the cheroot between his teeth and breathed a little tobacco-scented air through it.

"Batson?" Billy reminded him. "What do you know about this person?"

"Not a thing more than you do, boss. It's just a name to me."

"And those two out there, who would say anything if they thought it would keep them out of prison, are the ones who claim some SOB named Leo Batson is our Mail Bomber."

"That's about the size of it," Longarm agreed.

"And you believe them?"

"I don't say that I believe them or that I don't."

"But you think they could be telling the truth, here," Billy persisted.

"I think it's worth looking into," Longarm said. "I think we don't know shit about this Mail Bomber. I think that girl out there has the tools it takes to get information if she wants to. I think any deal we make with those two . . . if we make one at all . . . should be contingent on us finding this Batson person and him being the Mail Bomber."

"Contingent," Billy repeated in a soft, reflective tone of voice. "I didn't realize you knew any big words like that, Custis."

"Fuck you." Longarm smiled and added, "Sir."

"You do have a point though. We could make it clear that if they are trying to take us down the primrose path, we would add another charge to the time that is already facing them."

"How about they enter a conditional guilty plea with

14

the understanding that those charges will be dropped if and when we determine Batson is our man?"

"You're a real hard case, Long."

"Yes, but I'm lovable. Ask anybody."

"It might be worth a try. The postmaster general is raising holy hell with the attorney general over these bombings. And you know how that goes."

"Sure," Longarm said. "Some politician in Washington gets a knot in his dauber and everybody down the line has to turn himself inside out trying to untie it."

"Exactly. The attorney general does not like being pestered by someone he considers beneath his own exalted station. So he is pestering the hell out of the U.S. attorney here. And that worthy gentleman in turn is . . . shall I say it, Longarm?"

"Don't bother. I can see the boot marks on the back of your head every time you turn around, from where he's walking all over you."

"Which means all of us will be happier when we find this Mail Bomber," Billy said.

"Batson could be him."

"Or not." Vail leaned back in his chair, steepled his fingertips, and poked himself in the chin with them.

The Mail Bomber—Leo Batson or someone else—was a real pain in the ass. The man was a robber who appeared out of nowhere, sometimes on a train, sometimes stopping a stagecoach, sometimes stepping inside a post office or postal contract station. He had hit them all at different times.

He would help himself to whatever cash was available—he wasn't so loony that he would turn that down—but his main emphasis seemed to be on the destruction of the mail itself.

The son of a bitch would set fire to piles of loose mail if the place he chose to hit was a post office, but he took his name from his preferred hunting ground, which was

15

the road. He liked to take mail pouches, those heavy canvas, very nearly indestructible bags that mail is transported in, poke small holes in them, and insert sticks of dynamite in with the mail they contained.

The man did not make any attempt to look through the mail for money or other valuables. He just blew it up.

No one knew why the crackpot SOB did that. For whatever reason, or for no reason at all, he liked to blow the shit out of the U.S. mail.

The first occurrence had been almost ten months ago near Durango. Since that time, and with increasing frequency, he had stolen and/or destroyed mail in western and northern Colorado, in southern Wyoming and in western Nebraska. A traveling man was this unknown Mail Bomber.

Unknown, that is, until now. Maybe.

Billy turned his swivel chair around and stared out the window for several long moments. Then he turned back around and nodded. "Let's go see the U.S. attorney. And bring your friends along, please."

Chapter 4

"I can't promise you that Leo Batson is his real name," Cherie said. "That is the name he gave me, but I know that when he travels he uses different names."

"You aren't giving us much," Charles White said. White was the assistant U.S. attorney. He was straitlaced, always impeccably dressed, and something of a prude. He and Deputy Marshal Long had absolutely nothing in common. But White knew his job, and Longarm respected that.

"I'm telling you the truth," Cherie responded. "If that isn't good enough for you, then the hell with you." She looked ready to get up and flounce out of White's office.

Frankie grabbed her by the wrist and held her in the chair. After all, "out" from the prosecutor's office would mean "in" a jail cell. He was not about to let her peevishness land him behind bars.

"Both of us know Batson well enough to recognize him," Frankie put in. "Even when he is traveling under one of his phony names . . . what do you call those?"

"An alias, do you mean?"

"Right. One of those. Anyway, even when he isn't using the name Batson, we know each other."

17

"Both of you know him?"

"I've met him a couple times," Frankie said. "It's Cherie that knows him well. As you might, uh, understand."

"She fucked him?"

Longarm was surprised to hear the term come out of Charles White's mouth. The man did not cuss. Ever. Probably went dutifully to church every Sunday. Now he went and used a nasty word like that. What *was* the world coming to?

Frankie looked mildly taken aback, too. And he did not really know White. "I would not know what Batson and Miss Johnson chose to do in private," he said quite primly.

Johnson. Longarm hadn't heard Cherie's last name before. If indeed that was it. Leo Batson was not the only one able to change names when he jolly well wanted to.

"Miss Johnson?" White asked.

She stayed where she was—Frankie was not giving her any choice about that—but she was still unhappy. She gave White a haughty look and kept her pretty mouth shut.

"Miss Johnson, did you fuck Leo Batson?"

"That is none of your business," she snapped.

White looked at Longarm and shook his head. "I'm sorry, Marshal. I know your intentions are good here, but I cannot force anyone to help us if they are unwilling. Go ahead and take these two down to the lockup, then come back and we can go through the charges against them."

"Jesus, no," Frankie blurted.

"Oh, calm down. He's just trying to scare us," Cherie told him. Her voice was firm and her chin was held defiantly high.

Longarm shrugged. He stood and boosted Frankie off his chair with a tight grip on the skinny fellow's elbow. He did not have to encourage Cherie. She was on her feet

18

and more than ready to make an exit from that nasty old prosecutor's office.

Longarm wondered what Billy was going to say when Longarm got back to his office. When the marshal had left the room everything had been going fine. Now this.

He took the two downstairs, booked them into holding cells, and instructed the jailer to keep them in transient quarters, as they would probably be transferred to the Denver County Jail within the next day or two. He left them there, Frankie shaking and Cherie angry, and went back up to White's office.

"Are you shitting those two," Longarm asked the assistant U.S. attorney, "or are you serious?"

White smiled. "Let's just say we are giving them an opportunity to reflect upon the possibilities here."

"Think there might be anything to their Batson story?"

The lawyer shrugged. "Who knows? But if we are grasping at straws here, then let's take up a whole handful and see what comes of it."

"You'll drop the charges against them?"

"If they are sincere, of course."

"And if they aren't?"

"They will rue the day," White said. "Both of them."

Chapter 5

Charles White apparently was willing to start the cooking process if Frankie and Cherie did indeed want to stew in their own juices. He kept them sitting in a jail cell over the weekend before again bringing them to his office.

The two sat as they had before, but this time they were both disheveled and more than a little grimy, after the rather primitive facilities in the cells. Cherie did not look so defiant this morning. Frankie looked even shakier than he had before.

"Decide," White told them bluntly. "Cooperate or face immediate trial. I will be glad to prosecute you two. On the other hand, I would be every bit as happy to represent your interests before the court and appeal to the judge for a reduction of sentence. In fact, if you cooperate fully, we could drop most of the charges against you and see to it that you serve no prison time at all on the remaining charges. If I so recommend, the judge will sentence you to unsupervised probation. Do you understand what I am telling you, here?"

"We understand," Frankie said.

"I need to hear both of you say it," White told them. He sat patiently staring at Cherie. After a few moments she nodded her head. "What was that?" White prodded.

"I understand," Cherie grumbled in a low and reluctant voice. "I understand, damn you."

"Fine," White said cheerfully, choosing to ignore Cherie's pouting. "Now please tell us where we can find this Leo Batson who you claim is the Mail Bomber."

"I thought you understood," Frankie said. "We don't know where to look for him. Not just up and go see him. It's like . . . it's like him and us travel the same ground. Hunt the same territory, so t' speak. We never know when we'll see him or exactly where. But we run inta each other fairly regular. When we do, we're friendly, then we go our way and Leo, he goes his until the next time."

"Does this Batson always engage the, um, services of Miss Johnson, here?"

"He likes her real good. Has right from the first time. She is . . . like I told your marshal here . . . she has this special way about her. Once she's with a man, he's always wanting more." Frankie smirked and added, "You should try her out yourself, Your Honor."

"I am a married man, thank you."

"Most of 'em are."

"Be that as it may, I have no interest in taking you up on that offer. Furthermore, it could be construed as attempted bribery. Yet another charge that can be placed against you." White leaned back in his chair and smiled. "But we are looking for ways to eliminate those charges." He sat forward over the desk, his expression solemn. "*If* you cooperate."

"You know damn good and well we're gonna cooperate. You don't give us any choice 'bout that."

"Oh, you always have that other choice available to you. It is not a very good one, of course. Jail versus freedom. But you do have the choice. Now! I need you to tell us how we can find Batson."

"Your Honor . . ."

"I am not a judge, only a prosecutor."

"Yes sir, Your Honor, whatever you say."

"Go on then, please."

"Like I was saying a minute ago, there's no set place that we can say 'you go here an' look for a man with this appearance or that name.' If you see what I mean."

"Then how do you propose to help us take this man into custody?"

"Why, there's only one way that I can think of," Frankie said. "Cherie an' me will have to lead you to him. Get out there in our usual way an' act as bait, you might say. Quick as Leo sees Cherie, he'll come sniffing around her. He won't be able to help himself. He's got it bad for Cherie, y'see. Got it bad. You can nab him quick as he does that."

Honor among thieves, Longarm thought. He was seated at the side of the room, keeping his ears open and his mouth shut. Honor among thieves, indeed. If Leo Batson had to go down in order for Frankie and Cherie to avoid jail, well, that was tough on Leo, but so be it.

"There must be some way available that would not require your, um, direct participation. In the field, I mean. Some place you can tell us. Some name and description Long and the other deputies can use to find this man."

"There isn't none that I can think of," Frankie said. "Put us out there. Use us as bait. You'll get your man."

"I'm not sure about this," White said. "It would involve allowing you to remain free and not under physical restraint. Allowing you to travel. Having our deputies travel with you." He frowned, "I just do not know if the United States attorney for this district would agree to such a plan."

"I don't know of no other way it'd work," Frankie insisted.

"Long? Have you any thoughts on this matter?" White asked.

"Oh, not me, your honor." He grinned. "I'm just a passenger on this coach. You're the one doing the driving."

White frowned again. "I shall have to take this up with the proper authorities. I expect we will have an answer for you in another day or two."

"Day or two?" Cherie barked, coming out of her sulk long enough to become angry. "You want us to sit in those lousy cells for another day or two, while you drink tea with some high and mighty son of a bitch? You want us to rot, while you take your time deciding what's to become of us, damn you?"

"Yes, I do," White calmly told her. "For a day or two. Deputy Long, would you please escort these two downstairs again? Be sure they are given our finest rooms, would you?"

"A day or damn two," Cherie was muttering, as Longarm led them out into the corridor and toward the stairs. "Damn day or two."

Frankie was silent but seemed satisfied enough.

For his part, Longarm was thinking nothing was likely to come of this. The U.S. attorney surely would not want to let this unsavory pair go wandering around Colorado, Wyoming, and Nebraska at the government's expense, just on the off chance that they might encounter Leo Batson along the way. And that Batson might be the Mail Bomber.

No sir, Longarm figured, that was not very likely to happen.

Chapter 6

"We have to do it," Billy Vail said. "We have no choice. If it is grasping at straws . . . and of course that is exactly what it is . . . then we have to grab for every straw we can."

"I got to tell you, boss, I'm surprised," Longarm told him.

"I would be too, except we received word late yesterday afternoon of another robbery and bombing incident. The Mail Bomber, who may or may not be Batson, held up the mail car on a Union Pacific train yesterday in western Nebraska. There was a guard riding on the car. The cheeky damned Mail Bomber stole the man's watch and whatever cash he had on him, then took the mail pouch out onto bare ground beside the station platform.

"Then in full view of several dozen bystanders, Long, he dynamited the pouch. Four sticks, I am told. The telegraphed reports suggest the results were quite spectacular. Scraps of paper flying everywhere. The children in the crowd were cheering for him to do it again. Can you imagine that?" Billy sounded indignant, as if he were personally offended by the Mail Bomber's actions.

Well, in a way he probably was, Longarm realized.

After all, it was Billy and his deputies who were supposed to keep the peace and insure that no criminals or crazies played loose and free with the United States government. The Mail Bomber was thumbing his nose at the Post Office and, by extension, the entire U.S. government. At Marshal Vail, Custis Long, and every other federal lawman, too.

"There was a meeting last night," Billy said. "You might be interested to know that Charles White was opposed to the idea of, shall we say, employing the services of June Ann Johnson and Frank Powell."

"June Ann? Is that her real name?"

"Apparently."

"No wonder she changed it," Longarm said, reaching for a cheroot. He remembered in time that Billy did not want the smell of cigar smoke in his office and settled for gnawing on it for the moment, instead.

"What was I saying? Oh, yes. White thinks your pair will say anything in the hope they can avoid jail. He thinks they should be prosecuted and sent away for as long as the law allows."

"And his boss?" Longarm asked.

"The United States attorney has already wired Washington to assure them that we have a solid lead on the Mail Bomber, and that we are already in hot pursuit of the miscreant."

"We are?"

Billy shrugged. "As far as the postmaster general is concerned we are. The attorney general will have told him so by now."

"This hot pursuit meaning Frankie and Cherie?"

"I am afraid so."

"D'you think there is any chance they could be telling the truth? Or even what rightly or wrongly they really think is the truth?"

"Very little chance," Billy said. "But they are all we

have at the moment, so they are what we will use. If nothing else, it will allow us to send smoke signals to Washington."

"You know, of course, that the two of them will likely sneak away first chance they get?"

"We intend to make that difficult, if not impossible," Billy said. "Or should I say 'you' will make it difficult."

"Me?"

"You are the one who brought them here, deputy. They are yours to follow up on now."

"Thank you ever so much, boss," Longarm said, his voice heavy with sarcasm.

"You will have help," Billy said.

"Some new guy that I don't know? I know all your experienced deputies are already out in the field working other cases. Who else is available?"

"Your partner will not be one of our own people," Billy said.

Longarm chewed on the end of his cheroot and waited for the boss to continue.

"Because of the presence of a, um, female subject, the U.S. attorney feels it would be . . . inappropriate . . . to have a male officer watch Miss Johnson."

"Appropriate or not, Billy, there ain't no female officers."

"Perhaps not, but the U.S. attorney, at the urging of Charles White, has an alternative in mind."

Longarm raised an eyebrow but refused to rise to the bait Billy Vail was so obviously throwing out. He kept his mouth closed and waited.

After a moment Billy said, "You, Mr. Powell, and Miss Johnson will be accompanied by a matron from the women's prison system."

"You got to be shitting me, boss."

"Not at all. We found a suitably qualified person in Wyoming. She was notified of her assignment by wire last night and should be on her way here already."

"You're out of your minds. All of you. Sending a prison matron to act as a deputy? That's crazy."

"Not as crazy as you might think," Billy said. "And she will not be required to act as if she were a sworn deputy. Her duties will essentially be unchanged from what she normally does. She will keep watch over June Ann Johnson to insure the girl does not sneak away. She will accompany Miss Johnson at all times. *All* times. Even when in the restroom. You, of course, will do the same with Powell. The man is not to be out of your sight for a single moment."

"Why such close surveillance, Billy?" Longarm asked. "It isn't like either of us really believes anything is gonna come of this. Far as I can tell it's all an effort to throw dust in the eyes of those assholes back east in Washington City, so why should we care if one or both of them does eventually slip away. The charges against them are picayune. I mean, it ain't like they are a danger to society or anything. T' tell you the truth, boss, I only carried things this far because they went an' brought up the Mail Bomber. I wasn't expecting anything like that. An', well, maybe I was a little bit pissed off too that they thought they could brace me like that. Frankie an' his silly little pepperbox. He embarrassed me, dammit. But the charges against them, those are crap charges, not worth getting fussed up about."

"Oh, I see your point, Deputy. I might even agree with it. But this part is at the insistence of Charles White."

"What does he have to say about it?"

"Charles raised the question of whether Powell and Johnson might genuinely know the Mail Bomber . . . not an impossibility, of course, and not necessarily someone using the name Batson if they do know him . . . and intend to warn him about our efforts to apprehend him."

"Shit, Billy, the Mail Bomber already knows we want his ass in jail. He has to."

"Of course he does, but Charles became very upset with the idea of sending Powell and Johnson out to find our man. I think he wants to prosecute both of them and does not want to take any chance of their escape."

"Even if every word they've told us turns out to be the gospel truth," Longarm said, "the Mail Bomber wouldn't come near them if we got them in handcuffs."

"You are instructed to give all outward appearances of normalcy," Billy said.

"And if something goes wrong an' we happen to lose our bait before Batson snaps it up?"

"Then it will be your head on the block, of course, not Charles's."

"Politics as usual, is that it?"

"Cover your ass, Longarm. That is a rule that is as old as time and one that everyone in public office understands very, very well."

Longarm sighed. "Can I request t' be assigned to something else, boss? I don't like any part of this. The U.S. attorney covering his ass against the attorney general. The attorney general covering his ass against the postmaster general. White covering his ass with his boss out here. Billy, whoever has this assignment will be the only one with his ass hanging out in the breeze, and I just don't want it t' be me."

"You are certainly welcome to make that request, Longarm. After all, you are my senior deputy. I will quite naturally listen to your comments."

"Boss, I am hereby requesting to be relieved of this assignment. Put somebody else on it, if you don't mind."

"Very well, Deputy Long. I have received your request. But as you yourself pointed out just a few minutes ago, everyone else is already busy elsewhere. I'm afraid that I must deny your request. The job is yours." He pulled his watch out of his vest pocket and checked the time. "Good. Miss Bradbury's train should be arriving in forty minutes. If you hurry, there is time for you to get to the station to meet her."

"Miss Bradbury would be this jail matron from Wyoming?"

Billy smiled. "Exactly. A perfectly nice woman, I am sure. You two will no doubt get along famously."

Longarm scowled.

"Hurry along now, Longarm. You wouldn't want to miss meeting your partner, now would you?"

Chapter 7

Ruby Bradbury's train was on time, but Longarm saw no passenger who might reasonably be a prison matron from Wyoming. There were a pair of young women traveling together, who he was sure were on their way to new work assignments at some whorehouse or other. A trio of fluttering females, a little girl aged three or so, her mother and a woman Longarm guessed was the mother's mother. The young mother was so homely it was an amazement any man would do her the favor of giving her the tumble that resulted in the child. Who was a very pretty little thing, despite her ancestry. And there was a tall, elegant woman with red hair and a parasol. Longarm could not figure her out. From the way she was dressed she could be the wife of some wealthy industrialist . . . or the owner of that whorehouse the pair of youngsters were going to.

Longarm kept waiting for a jail matron to emerge from the train, but he saw nothing on the order of the beefy, florid, hard-faced creature he expected to meet and be teamed with.

Ruby Bradbury, he thought, would be drab as a mud hen and have shoulders like a coal miner. Probably the complexion of a coal miner, too. She would smell of lye

31

soap and cornstarch and wear her hair skinned back so tight it would turn the corners of her eyes up. Oh, he knew what prison matrons looked like. Lord knew he'd seen enough of them in his time. They were scary things, those matrons.

So where the hell was this one?

Longarm waited with growing impatience while the train conductor helped folks down onto the platform— fewer and fewer of them until finally no more emerged, and the conductor picked up the metal steps and motioned to the engineer to get underway again.

The train chuffed and clanked and began to pull away, without any sign of Ruby Bradbury.

Now what?

Longarm checked his watch. There was no logical reason for him to do that, he realized even as he was doing it. It did not matter a tinker's damn what time it was. The train had come and now was going, and knowing the time would do nothing to influence Miss Bradbury.

The woman had simply failed to show up, that was all. She must have missed the train in Cheyenne. Probably off buying a bushel basket of fried chicken to munch on during the journey, Longarm rather uncharitably thought. After all, the ugly old bat might prefer a peck of candy to a bushel of crispy drumsticks.

Women! Damn them one and damn them all. If it hadn't been for that damned Cherie Johnson swishing her cute ass under his nose, he wouldn't be in this mess now. If he wanted to look at it that way, it was his own fault, but . . .

"Sir?"

Longarm turned, a scowl still on his face. The tall lady was standing there. A few men remained on the platform. The female family threesome had disappeared, along with most of the other passengers, and the two over-powdered floozies were negotiating something with a cab driver.

Longarm could just imagine what that negotiation would entail. And its outcome. Very likely the hansom driver would carry the two girls and their grips to their new place of employment in exchange for a blow job inside his rig. At the moment Longarm would have been happy enough to be a cab driver himself. And that sentiment had nothing to do with free blow jobs. Whatever *was* he going to tell Billy Vail about this Bradbury battle-ax?

"Sir?" the tall woman repeated.

"Oh. Sorry. I was, uh, thinking about something else." Longarm yanked his hat off and stifled an impulse to bow and make a leg. Who the hell did that sort of thing in these modern times?

Up close the woman was even more impressively handsome than she had been from across the platform. She wore a bottle-green traveling gown with a pale and very lightweight duster over it, a feathered hat cocked to one side, and a half veil shielding her eyes.

Exceptionally pretty eyes, Longarm could see despite the veil. They were a very pale . . . gray? Green? He could not decide. She had a long, slender neck, patrician nose, high and rounded cheeks, delicate ears. Her hair was that dark, rich shade of red that he thought was properly termed auburn.

She was tall enough that she looked at him eyeball to eyeball when she stood before him on the railroad depot platform.

And her carriage, her bearing, were such that she could make a claim to the royal blood of continental Europe and he would accept her word without question.

"How can I help you, miss? Ma'am. Uh, how can I help you?" He felt shy as a schoolboy with a crush on his teacher.

"I was expecting to be met and . . . forgive me if I am wrong . . . but you fit the description of the gentleman who was supposed to meet me here this morning."

"Miss, I cannot believe there is in all of Denver a cad so foolish as to leave you standing on this platform all by your lonesome. Mayhap I can be of service?"

"Do you happen to know a deputy marshal Custis Long, sir?"

"Miss?"

"My name is Ruby Bradbury." She smiled and extended her hand in a hearty shake. "I believe you and I will be working together."

Longarm grinned. Maybe he should rush in and give old Billy a big hug quick as they got over to the Federal Building. It was looking like this might turn out to be a pretty interesting assignment after all.

Chapter 8

"Like hell we will!" Cherie Johnson shrieked when Charles White told her about the plan. "If you think we're gonna have a bunch of strangers hanging over us day an' night . . ."

"You can always go to jail instead," White said. "The choice is entirely yours."

The threat shut Cherie up. It did nothing to make her any happier with the arrangement.

"The deal is this. No . . . and I do mean that there will be *no* activity that does not include Marshal Long or Matron Bradbury. If one of you wakes in the night and needs to use the outhouse, you will wake your respective partner and have him or her accompany you. Violate that agreement, and you will be on your way behind bars. Both of you. Are we clear on this? If one of you fails to meet our requirements, then both of you face trial and incarceration."

"Like after we get a fair trial you'll hang us?" Cherie snapped.

White was unperturbed. "Exactly."

"You bastard."

"Perhaps so, but I will not risk letting the two of you

do or say anything that would tip off this Batson about our activities."

"See here, now," Frankie said. "We are the ones who informed you about Leo to begin with. How can you fail to trust us now?"

"It is one thing for you to make an offer of cooperation when you are in imminent danger of imprisonment," White responded. "It is another for you to continue cooperating afterward. I've seen it time and time again. Someone is desperate to evade a long prison term, so he offers more than he can produce. Then he has second thoughts. Will the person he is giving up to the law retaliate? Will other criminals learn that he is a snitch and take revenge? I see these things happen all too often. I will not risk seeing it again with the two of you." White stood and glared down at Frankie and Cherie. "So make up your minds. You cooperate fully, including this close supervision by Marshal Long and Matron Bradbury, or we take you right back downstairs. And keep you there."

"I don't like this," Cherie moaned.

"You are not required to like it. You are required only to do it."

"What about our, um, sleeping arrangements?" Frankie asked. "Surely we will not be watched overnight." He reached for Cherie's hand, making it clear what he meant by the question.

"You will sleep in the same room as Marshal Long," White told him. "Miss Johnson will sleep with Matron Bradbury."

"But . . ."

"No argument," White said crisply. "That is the way it is going to be. Period."

Frankie squeezed Cherie's hand and gave her a look that quite clearly was a promise that they would find time alone together.

Not that Longarm could blame Frankie Powell for his

interest. Cherie was quite the cutie. Hell, Longarm had wanted a piece of her, too. That was what got all of them into this mess. He still wouldn't mind it if things were different.

For that matter, Longarm would be pleased to find himself making the beast with two backs with Cherie Johnson *or* with Ruby Bradbury. The two were as different as night and day. But a man can enjoy the pleasures of both night and daytime, can't he?

"There's something I oughta bring up," Frankie said, still holding onto Cherie's hand. "If you want this thing to work, I mean."

"Of course we want it to work," White said. Which was not to say that anyone actually expected it to. But it would certainly be nice if it did.

"Then you gotta let Cherie an' me do something with these two," Frankie said, waving his free hand in the direction of Longarm and Miss Bradbury.

"Do something," White repeated. "Do what exactly?"

"They ain't exactly dressed like the kind me and Cherie would get friendly with. They look . . . shit, they look proper." Frankie managed to make the word "proper" sound thoroughly improper. "You know what I mean?"

"No," White admitted.

"Look, we go waltzing into one of our hangouts with these two looking like they do and everybody will know there's something wrong. It won't look natural like."

"Everybody?" White asked.

Frankie shrugged. "Not the sheep. Fool sheep won't see nothing. They never do. But the people who count, the people like us and Leo Batson, they'll all see it. There won't any of them come close to us while we're with Mister Tall an' Handsome here or Lady Butter Wouldn't Melt in Her Mouth."

"What do you propose?" White asked.

"Before we take a step toward finding Leo, you gotta let Cherie and me make a few changes."

"I think we can allow that," White said.

"Hey, dammit!" Longarm protested.

But his protests, and those of Ruby Bradbury's, were ignored by Charles White and the U.S. attorney, and for that matter by Billy Vail, too. In the end it was a completely renovated—and completely unhappy—Custis Long who walked with Frankie Powell onto the railroad platform.

Chapter 9

Longarm wished there was a bush he could hide behind. Or a hole he could crawl into. He felt that miserable, felt like everyone for a block in any direction was staring at him.

If he wasn't allowed to wear his usual tweed coat and corduroy trousers, then why not trail clothes? He was comfortable in trail clothes. Wore them all the time when he was out doing rough work in rough country. Jeans and a vest, that would have been just fine. But . . .

He stood there on the railroad platform, exposed to the whole damned world in a cheap, badly cut brown linen jacket that was fading to a blotchy, ugly yellow on the left shoulder. His britches were a rusty red-brown color. He wore shoes instead of boots. And—worst of all by far—there was a derby hat perched above his ears.

A derby, for Pete's sake. Damn thing looked to him like a spittoon turned upside-down.

"So don't look into any mirrors," Frankie Powell advised him when Longarm began grumbling about the derby.

"I have to shave sometimes, don't I?"

"With your hat on?"

Longarm shut up. But he hated the derby. Stupid looking thing.

"If you want anybody to believe you're with us you have to dress the part," Frankie insisted.

"What about my revolver?"

"What about it?"

"Won't people see it if I wear it like this?"

"They see it now, don't they?"

"Yes, but . . ."

"Nobody will be worried about that. People in our line of work, some of them anyway, do use guns from time to time."

"Don't tell me you think that peashooter of yours is a real gun?" Longarm said scornfully. Frankie's pepperbox had been a bone of contention among them. He claimed his use of it was too well known for him to leave it behind and have someone become suspicious.

The ugly little weapon, extremely heavy for its small size, was in Frankie's coat pocket now, dragging that side of the coat slightly off his scrawny shoulder. Which did, Longarm admitted, give some credibility to the man's claim that his friends would notice if the gun were not there.

At Longarm's suggestion they had reached a compromise that Charles White found acceptable. Frankie kept his gun. But Longarm unscrewed the nipples and threw them away, leaving the pepperbox intact but making it impossible to fit a percussion cap in place, even if the barrels were charged. Impossible short of buying more of the steel nipples, that is, and Frankie would not be going into any gun shops without Longarm watching over him, so that should not matter.

Longarm found his new duds, worn as directed by Frankie Powell, embarrassing.

He found Ruby Bradbury's positively hilarious.

The elegant jailer had been made over by Cherie John-

40

son so that she looked like a tart in search of a sugar daddy.

She had on a bright, bright red dress cut so low it was an amazement that her tits didn't fall out of it, high-heeled shoes that made her look even taller than she already was, and a very large and very poorly made cameo suspended on a slightly grubby ribbon at her otherwise regal throat.

She wore makeup, too. Powder and rouge and some sort of red goop on her lips and a smudge of dark soot brushed on above each eyelid, and her hair was not so meticulously coifed as it was to begin with. Cherie had done something to it so that wisps of auburn hair escaped here and there from beneath the brim of a black hat with one long, broken feather drooping over the back of Ruby's neck. The hat had seen better days and made Ruby look as if she had, too.

Longarm withheld any comments he might have made comparing her with a circus clown. But if he'd known the woman better she would have been in for some raucous ribbing indeed.

The funny thing though was that as silly as she looked, Cherie's changes made Longarm want to pick Ruby up, throw her over his shoulder, and carry her off to the nearest bed. Or couch. Or, hell, just fling her down on the depot platform planks and do her there.

She was . . . he thought about it for a bit. She was touchable now. Or looked touchable, anyway. In her own clothing she'd seemed elegant but distant, even slightly unreal. Now, slightly mussed and a little bedraggled, she looked like a woman who would put on airs, but who would lift her skirts if the price was right.

Longarm had to wonder if Frankie's efforts with him were as effective as Cherie's were with Ruby.

The truth, of course, was that Longarm himself was in no position to judge that.

But Cherie certainly knew what she was doing when

41

she dressed Ruby for her role. Longarm hoped Frankie was as good when it came to his own appearance. Idiot fucking derby and all.

Longarm pulled out his watch and checked the time. The train should be along any minute now, and they would be boarding soon.

For whatever good it would do, which was probably none. But Charles White was able to assure the U.S. attorney who could report to the attorney general who could get the asshole postmaster general off his back. That was the important thing. Wasn't it?

Chapter 10

"Hyde's Junction. Next stop Hyde's Junction." The conductor repeated his information over and over in a sing-song voice as he made his way through the string of four passenger coaches.

The railroad cars swayed and bumped over the slightly uneven tracks, but the conductor walked as easily as a sailor striding the shifting deck of a ship at sea. And just as on a ship, the passengers had to grab hold of solid objects in order to keep their balance if they wanted to walk the aisles.

Frankie came back from the privy closet, using the seat backs as anchors, moving left to right and back again. He leaned up against a seat occupied by a pair of drunks and let the conductor pass, then resumed his journey back to the seats where Longarm and the ladies waited. Frankie claimed a sour stomach and had made three trips to the shitter since they pulled out of Cheyenne. Longarm just hoped the sleazy little son of a bitch was not leaving notes or somehow passing messages intended to give the game away.

Not that Longarm really expected anything to come of

43

this stupid venture anyway, but if he was going to be in it then he intended to give it his best shot.

"Hyde's Junction, that's our stop," Frankie said as he squeezed past Longarm's knees and dropped into the grimy, soot-stained seat next to the window.

"What the hell is at a dead-ass, nowhere place like Hyde's Junction?" Longarm asked. He had been through the tiny community more times than he could possibly remember, but the only thing he could think of the trains ever stopping there for was water and wood.

Frankie gave him a smug, "I know things that you don't" sort of look, but said nothing.

Neither of the ladies said anything either, and may not have heard him, for just about then the steam whistle on the locomotive shrieked and the brakemen began tightening the brake shoes, adding that grinding squeal to the din.

Ruby and Cherie were in the seat immediately in front of the one occupied by Longarm and Frankie. Like Longarm, Ruby was in the aisle seat, the better to control her prisoner.

From his seat Longarm could see the top of Cherie's head as it barely cleared the back of the seat. Ruby, on the other hand, sat head and shoulders above the top of the padded bench. The tip end of her hat feather drooped over onto Longarm's side of the seat, bobbing and bouncing with every movement of the coach. Damn thing was positively hypnotic, drawing his attention back to it over and over again in spite of his efforts to keep from staring at it.

He saw Cherie's head turn. She must have said something to Ruby, because the matron leaned down to listen to her, then nodded. Probably telling Ruby that they would be getting off at Hyde's Junction, Longarm guessed.

The train whistle screamed again, and the brakes began

to have an effect on the enormous weight of the train. They began to slow, the interval between clicks, as the wheels passed over the track joints, perceptibly longer now.

Hyde's Junction indeed. Getting off here would be a first experience for Longarm. He didn't even think there was a platform to receive disembarking passengers. As best he could remember, they would have to step down onto bare ground.

The train ground and shuddered its way to a halt, and Longarm stood to retrieve his carpetbag from the rack overhead. He was traveling light. No Winchester. No saddle. No hope to accomplish anything. The only thing positive about any of this was that he was doing what Billy Vail needed done. And there wasn't much he would not be willing to do for Billy.

A porter appeared as if by magic to fetch down Ruby's and Cherie's bags, and Longarm stepped back so he could keep an eye on Frankie while that gentleman got his own damn bag.

The four of them, Longarm noticed, were the only passengers who were taking any interest whatsoever in Hyde's Junction. He thought about inspecting the privy closet to make sure Frankie hadn't left any notes behind, but there wasn't time for that. It would take only a moment for the train crew to dump a fresh supply of water into the steam locomotive's tank, and they all had to be clear of the train when it pulled away again.

He and Frankie trailed meekly along behind the women, who were in turn following the porter.

They disembarked—onto a platform, not gravel; so much for the powers of memory—and were left standing, while the train almost immediately chuffed away on its eastward journey.

"Now what?" Longarm asked.

Chapter 11

"Gimme a dollar," Frankie said.

"What?"

"I need a dollar."

"You're out of your mi . . ."

"Look, we got to check into the hotel, don't we? I need a dollar to do that. You pay in advance. That's the rule. No exceptions."

"I was gonna give them an expense voucher."

Frankie rolled his eyes, and Cherie shook her head sadly, as if she were viewing the antics of a half-wit.

"If you want to blow this whole deal, go ahead an' use your voucher then. But every skimmer and scammer this side of the Mississippi is gonna know about it before sundown tomorrow."

"I hadn't thought . . ."

"And don't be thinking," Frankie interrupted again, "that you can let on that you and me are sharing a room an' the girls in another. They know me here, an' they know Cherie is my piece. We always take one room together, the two of us. So I take one room and you take the other. Who sleeps where is none of their business, but if you don't want tongues to wag, you'll do this like I

47

say. Now give me the damn dollar, will you?"

Longarm dug into his pocket and discovered that he had precious few dollars there. When he was traveling at the government's expense, he always came prepared with vouchers that he could give. The merchant could present them for payment afterward. He had not expected to pay with cash out of his pocket for the travel and living expenses of four people, for crying out loud.

He looked at Ruby. "How are you fixed for cash money?"

She looked slightly taken aback. "I'm a jail matron, Deputy. I earn twenty-two fifty a month, for God's sake. How would you expect me to be fixed for cash."

"That bad, huh?"

She nodded.

Longarm shook his head. "Boys an' girls, we are gonna have to go easy on the spending. We're just starting out and already we're broke."

Cherie pouted but then with a sigh said, "I suppose I can turn a few tricks and pick up a little money."

"You mean like, uh . . . ?"

"I mean like I can fuck some guys, yes. Frankie doesn't like to share if he doesn't have to, but sometimes he has to. Or we can shake somebody down."

"Not here, of course," Frankie said quickly. "We wouldn't be welcomed back here ever again if we tried to take down somebody here."

"Besides," Cherie said, "anybody staying at Hyde's would just laugh at us if Frankie tried to pull the deal here. I mean, we're all scammers here, aren't we? Present company excepted, of course."

"Are you telling me that this hotel you want to check into is filled with criminals?"

"Yes. What kind of people did you think we would want to be around between jobs?" Frankie asked.

"I never . . . shit, what if somebody there knows me?"

"Then we're screwed."

"Or knows my name?" Longarm asked.

Frankie shrugged. "So who d'you want to be? You can be anybody you like and nobody will question it. Would you care to be Ulysses S. Grant for a little while?"

"I could . . ."

"Sure. Not that anybody would believe it, mind. But they'd all pretend to. We're a polite bunch that way."

"And no scamming or cheating allowed. Not even at cards," Cherie put in.

It was Longarm's turn to roll his eyes. Just what in hell had he gotten himself into here?

"What about you, Ruby?" Longarm asked. "Is anyone likely to know you or your name?"

"Probably not," the tall woman said. "But you they might have heard about. I certainly knew the name before, although I couldn't recognize you from what I'd heard. You really must change your name."

"Damn," Longarm mumbled. "In that case, I'll . . . okay, everybody. From now on I'm called Henry." He was thinking about Billy Vail's clerk back at the office. He liked Henry, so why not borrow his name?

"Last name? I'll be expected to introduce you to our, uh, friends," Frankie said.

"Oh . . . uh . . ."

"How about Smith?" Cherie suggested.

"Isn't that kind of obvious?" Longarm asked.

"Sure, but so what. Nobody will care. Besides, some people really are named Smith, and who's to know that you aren't one of them."

"All right then. Henry Smith it is," Longarm said.

"And remember. As far as everyone else is concerned, me and Cherie are together just like always. You and the oak here are your own couple."

"Oak?" Ruby asked.

"Big. Tall. Oak. You know?"

Ruby's expression said she did not especially like the allusion. But then, Longarm could not blame her for not liking any part of this assignment. After all, he did not like any of it, either.

But as for him coupling up with Ruby Bradbury, well, he could handle that if he had to.

"Ready?" he asked.

Frankie picked up Cherie's bag and his own. Longarm hesitated for a moment, then grabbed Ruby's bag so they, too, could go through the outwardly visible motions of being together. Damn!

"This way," Frankie said and strode off into what little there was of Hyde's Junction, Cherie trotting along at his heels like a well trained bird dog.

Longarm gritted his teeth and followed with Ruby, head held high, beside him, her hat feather bobbing in their wake.

Chapter 12

Hyde Inn. Longarm was beginning to think there was more to the name than just the designation for a hotel. Hide indeed. They hadn't yet crossed the lobby before he spotted two men who fit the descriptions of a pair who had held up a bank in Central City, Colorado.

Right now there was not a damn thing he could do about them. Under Billy Vail's strict orders. But he hadn't been told to ignore everything he saw while he was on this useless job. Just to pretend to. As soon as he was free to act again, he figured to come back to Hyde's Junction with a couple dozen federal, state, and local boys and see just what fell out when they shook this particular tree. The results might be kind of interesting.

For now though he was . . . what the hell was his name again? Oh, yes. For the time being he was Henry Smith, exact occupation undeclared, a close personal friend of Frankie Powell.

The innkeeper was a short, fat, happy-looking fellow named Ben Sanders. Frankie performed the introductions, then slapped onto the counter the silver dollar Longarm had given him over at the railroad depot.

"Two adjoining," Frankie said, as if he were in charge

of their little group. "Second floor, if you please."

Sanders chuckled. "I know, I know. You don't like to climb steps any better than I do."

"So d'you have two together, Ben?"

"For you, Frankie, sure. If I did not I would throw somebody out into the cold and the snow and the rain. You will be with us long?"

Frankie shrugged. "Depends, Ben. You know how that is. Is Leo around?"

"He was here two weeks ago. Said he'd be back, but he did not say when. But then you know how Leo is. Here one minute, gone the next."

"If he does come in, tell him we're here, would you?" Frankie winked. "Tell him Cherie misses him."

"How come Cherie never misses me, Frankie?"

"Shit, Ben, you never said anything 'bout being interested before."

"Yeah, but my wife wasn't back east visiting her kin before, neither." Ben gave Ruby a careful looking over. "Now there's the long and the short of things. I, uh, don't suppose we could arrange a party? A threesome?"

Longarm grabbed Ruby's arm before she could haul off and brain Sanders with a cuspidor. He squeezed. Hard.

Little white lines formed around Ruby's mouth from her pressing her lips so tightly together to keep from snapping the man's head off. But she was good. She kept those lips closed.

"I dunno, Ben. We'll wait and see what happens, okay?"

"Sure, Frankie. Sure thing." To Longarm he said, "No offense intended, Mr. Smith."

"None taken, Mr. Sanders."

"Call me Ben. Everybody does."

"And I'm Henry."

"Right. I don't know how you boys are fixed right now but if, um, if you and Frankie want to pick up a little extra, I'm sure I can work something out for your girls to do. If you want to, that is. There's no pressure at the Hyde Inn. Never. Frankie can tell you. No pressure at all."

"Thank you, Ben. That's good t' know."

Longarm felt Ruby shift position and for a moment thought she was going to go across the counter and rip Ben Sanders's throat out. He gave her arm another warning squeeze, but she was all right. He hoped.

He did find it kind of interesting though that neither Ben Sanders nor Frankie Powell thought it at all unusual that the discussion remain strictly among the men. Ruby and Cherie had no say in the matter. At least not out here in public they didn't. Apparently they were expected to be quiet and do whatever they were damn well told. *Any*-thing they were damn well told.

These folks, Longarm was beginning to learn, lived a very different sort of life from what others would consider to be normal.

Sanders took a pair of keys down from a rack on the wall behind him and handed them over.

"Good rooms," Frankie said, glancing at the numbers engraved on the key tags.

"Nothing but the best for my friends, you know," Ben told him with a salacious wink. He was wanting that threesome, all right.

Not that Longarm could blame him.

Frankie led the way upstairs, Cherie following meekly behind and Ruby trailing, although Longarm did not think there was anything the least bit meek about Ruby at the moment.

No, sir, if Ruby Bradbury were a tea kettle there would be steam coming out of her ears.

Not a bad-looking woman though, Longarm reflected. Even in that hat with the hideous feather bouncing behind her.

Chapter 13

They settled the girls in one room and the two males in the other. There was only one bed in each room, though, and the beds were not over-large.

"You can sleep on the floor," Longarm told Frankie.

"Say now, that isn't the way it's done. You have to share a bed in lots of hotels and . . ." Frankie saw the look on Longarm's face and shut his mouth. There are, after all, things that are worse than having to sleep on the floor. "Are you ready?" he asked instead.

"Ready for what?"

"Why, we have to go downstairs, don't we? Mingle with the other guests? It's the way Cherie and I always are when we come here. You don't want to make people suspicious, do you?"

"What I want to do is lock every fucking one of these people away, then burn the place down. That's what I want."

"What put you in such a bad mood?"

"I dunno, I . . . aw, shit. You're right. Reckon I am in a lousy mood all of a sudden. I don't know why."

Frankie shrugged it off and changed the subject.

"You'll need to give me some money before we go down, y'know."

"Money? What the hell for?"

"Drinks. Maybe a little cards. We have to keep everything looking normal, don't forget."

Longarm suspected Mr. Powell here would be more than happy to have himself a nice time at the government's expense. Frankie was not very good at what he did—after all, Longarm had seen the silly bastard in action and knew Frankie would be menacing only to the easiest of the sheep—and likely did not have money to throw around even at the best of times.

Still, he was under orders here. He and Ruby were indeed supposed to keep everything looking normal.

The only problem with that, of course, was that Longarm did not really know what normal was for these two. He was forced to take Frankie's word on it.

And wasn't that a laugh! Taking Frankie Powell's word. What the hell had he come to?

"All right, dammit. I'll give you a couple bucks. But put your meals and drinks on the room charges, so I can get a proper accounting when we check out. I want to get my money back on the expense sheet, and . . ."

"You can stop right there. This isn't Denver, you know. And the Hyde isn't exactly a real usual sort of hotel, anyway. Everything here is cash on the line. You can pay in advance for your room if you like, or you can pay every morning to keep the room that night. But any other service you pay for when you get it. Food, drinks, bath water, or whatever. You pay as you go. No tabs, no room charges."

"Even for you?"

"That's right, even for me. I know how things work here, and I wouldn't think of asking for anything different. Ben would think it damn funny if I did anything different now."

Longarm growled and mumbled a little, but he dug into his pocket.

"Give me ten dollars to start with," Frankie said.

"Get fucked. I'll give you two."

"I have to pay for our dinners, don't I? I'm supposed to be the host, sort of. Showing you and Ruby the ropes. So I have to pay."

"All right, I'll give you three."

"It isn't coming out of your pocket, y'know. Damn government can afford it."

"All right, five. But that's it."

"For this afternoon."

"For today."

"You're killing me."

Longarm gave the skinny gambler a long, level look. "Get outa line and I just may have t' do that, you know," he said softly.

Frankie went a little pale and stopped his whining. "I will, uh, I will check and see if the girls are ready." He went to the door that connected the two rooms and tapped very lightly on it, standing with his back to Longarm and doing his best to look like he was not rattled by the reminder that he and Cherie were not yet out of the woods with the law.

Chapter 14

Longarm didn't know what Ben Sanders's game was, but he did seem in his own way to be honest. A hideout—or in this case a Hyde Inn—devoted to criminals could be expected to extract big money from them for its services. It was said that receiving sanctuary inside Robbers' Roost would cost a man a thousand dollars a month, not including women and fresh horses.

But here at the Hyde, Sanders charged a very ordinary thirty-five cents for dinner, twenty for a light lunch, and a dime for pie and coffee.

The happy foursome took their dinner in the Hyde's dining room, along with a dozen or so other felons. Longarm did not know them. But they had the look about them that told him what they were.

He found it interesting that most did not appear to be criminals in the more violent trades. These, he suspected, were confidence artists, crooked gamblers, and sneak thieves with maybe a few pickpockets thrown in for good measure. Perhaps the armed robbers and safecrackers went elsewhere for their recreation.

Dinner consisted of roast pigeon in brown gravy, mashed potatoes, and apple sauce, and coffee or tea was included in the price of the meal. Cherie had the tea, the only one at their table who did so. But then she seemed to be in a mood to play the grand and gracious lady this evening. Showing off for her friends, Longarm supposed.

"After supper we can go into the bar," Frankie explained. "The girls can come with us." He laughed. "This isn't like some fancy-pants joint in the city. Every girl here plays, one way or another."

About a third of the men in the room were accompanied by women. And not a fat broad nor a real dog in the bunch. Longarm wondered exactly what Frankie meant when he said they "played." Did he mean they were all whores? One looked so prim she would faint at the mere mention of a dick, nevermind the sight of one. Or did Frankie mean they were involved in some sort of racket?

Probably the latter, Longarm decided. Women often do well as card sharps and shills. They could be useful to a crook in any number of ways, he supposed.

"Look, maybe we need to put in an appearance in there for appearance's sake," Longarm said in a soft voice that would not carry to the adjacent tables, "but we aren't gonna play like its old home week here. We'll show up. Have a drink. Then go upstairs to our rooms. Your friend Batson isn't here, and that's all we care about. Right?"

Frankie did not like it. But he nodded. Cherie rolled her eyes and pouted. Ruby remained impassive. To her this whole thing would be just a job, the sort of thing that would look good on her record when it came time for promotions to be passed around.

They finished eating—the food was really pretty good—and Frankie left a sizeable tip for the teenage girl who waited on their table. That would have been fine except that it was Longarm's money he was being so generous with. Bet the little bastard would've been tighter with his own cash, Longarm silently grumbled.

The bar was not so brightly lit as the dining room.

Cigar and pipe smoke swirled around the overhead lamps, and there was a low hum of conversation from the handful of guests who were gathered there.

"It will get livelier later on," Frankie said, as if he couldn't wait for that to happen. "No trouble, though. That's one of the rules. No one causes trouble here or he won't be allowed to come back. Wouldn't be popular with any of the other regulars, either."

"No shooting, stabbing, not even any brawling?" Longarm asked.

"Never. It isn't permitted, not any more than cheating at cards is allowed. You will find some of the finest deck mechanics this side of Chicago in this room. Not a one of them would think of rigging the cards inside these walls."

"Commendable of them, I'm sure," Longarm said in a dry, sarcastic voice.

The sarcasm passed right over Frankie's head. The skinny gambler beamed and nodded.

"I'll bring the drinks," Longarm said. "What does everybody want?"

"Nothing for me," Ruby said. But then she was on duty here and obviously did not intend to forget it.

"Champagne cocktail for me," Cherie piped up. Longarm could've predicted that. Seeing as how he was the one paying.

"Brandy if you please," Frankie said. Longarm couldn't decide if he too was trying to put on airs or if he really liked the stuff. Longarm decided to give Frankie the benefit of the doubt. Could be he really enjoyed brandy, which Longarm generally found a touch too syrupy for his own taste.

The others settled around a table off to one side of the room, and Longarm made his way to the bar, where a bald man with a truly magnificent mustache was pouring.

Longarm leaned an elbow on the polished mahogany

and settled in to wait until the barkeep was free to take their order.

Then he looked at the man standing next to him and all the blood drained from his face.

They were fucked. If this guy glanced in Longarm's direction the game was over and done with.

Shit! he inwardly screamed. What the hell was he supposed t' do now?

Chapter 15

Longarm had no idea what the man's original name had been, but nowadays he called himself J. Jimmy Jay, and he was one bad son of a bitch.

There was no telling what he was doing here surrounded by nonviolent criminals, but Jimmy Jay did not belong in that relatively benign category. Jimmy was, plain and simple, a hired killer. And a good one.

No, Longarm thought. "Good" was not the right word to describe him. He was anything but a good man. Effective. That certainly fit. He was one damned effective murderer for hire, wanted in half a dozen states. Hell, active as he'd been over the years, he might well be wanted in all the states.

Jimmy Jay had plied his nasty trade for more than a dozen years that Longarm knew of. And he would have been free to continue right on without any fear of federal peace officers, except for one glaringly huge mistake about six months previously.

He had been hired by the owner of a small stagecoach line in the south of Arizona Territory. The stage-line proprietor had visions of building an empire for himself. If only he could eliminate the competition. And instead of doing that by way of good business practice and efficient, low-cost service for his patrons, he decided to get a jump on the process by killing off the owners of three competing lines.

J. Jimmy Jay was duly hired. The coach-line owner told local authorities afterward that he had paid three hundred dollars up front and another thousand per head after the killings were done. And the killings were indeed done. Very efficiently from long range with one big, far-reaching son of a bitch of a rifle.

Unfortunately for the stagecoach man, the sudden demise of all three of his competitors laid the suspicions at his door. Even worse for the silly piece of shit, a little intense questioning—exact methods not discussed in polite company, nor in the presence of judges—led to a tearful confession. Tearful, Longarm assumed, not because he'd done it, but because he'd been caught.

That worthy gentleman was now sitting in a jail cell awaiting the necktie party that was scheduled in his honor in another month or two.

Normally the disclosure of Jimmy Jay's involvement as the fellow who pulled the trigger would have been of passing interest only. After all, he was already wanted in Arizona on at least three other charges. One more would hardly be enough to cause any excitement.

This string of murders, though, turned out to be as unfortunate for Jimmy Jay as they were for his employer. His third victim this time was a gent by the name of Harkin. Bill, Bob, something like that, Longarm recalled. And Mr. B. Harkin not only owned a small stage-line, he also held an appointment as postmaster of McCarthy, Arizona Territory.

That made the matter serious. Jimmy Jay had killed an employee of the United States Post Office and immediately become the subject of intense interest by federal peace officers.

Including deputy U.S. marshal Custis Long.

And now J. Jimmy Jay was standing next to him at a bar in Hyde's Junction.

Longarm recognized him immediately.

Just as Jimmy Jay would recognize Longarm, if the man so much as turned his head in this direction.

The two had met once before in southwestern Colorado, were introduced, even sat down at the same table as participants in a game of five-card stud. At the time Jay was not wanted by the feds. He seemed to get quite a kick out of sitting across the table from one of the top deputies in the United States Marshal's Service.

Now . . .

Shit!

If Longarm took Jimmy Jay down now, his cover would be blown, his orders violated, and any slight chance of grabbing Leo Batson would evaporate quick as a smoke ring puffed into the teeth of a blizzard.

If he did *not* take Jimmy Jay, God knew when Longarm or some other officer would get another chance. Or how many innocents would die in the meantime.

Longarm shifted position so that his back was toward Jimmy, but continued to keep an eye on him in the mirror behind the Hyde Inn's bar.

What the hell *was* he gonna do here!

Chapter 16

"Barkeep. You got one of those water closet things, so's a man can take a shit?"

"No, sir, sorry. All we have is the outhouse out back."

"No modern conveniences, huh? Damn."

The bartender shrugged and turned away, obviously not caring a whit if the customer liked it or not.

Longarm was much more interested. If Jimmy Jay was going out to the shitter, his problem might be solved.

As soon as Jay disappeared in the direction of the back of the hotel, Longarm followed. He paused at the back door to make sure Jay had plenty of time to find the outhouse and make himself comfortable in there. Then Longarm slipped out into the night.

He paused again to let his eyes adjust to the dim illumination given off by a rising quarter moon, then made his way carefully along the path that led from the back door to a dark shape that from its size looked like it must be a two-holer.

Perfect. He could walk right in and Jay would only think it was someone else who needed to relieve himself.

Longarm quit trying to be quiet and let his boots thump a little on the hard-packed earth of the path. When he got to the outhouse he reached for the door and pulled. The heavy, earthy scent of decomposing shit greeted him, and he wrinkled his nose.

He stepped inside, expecting to find Jimmy Jay sitting there with his britches around his ankles.

The outhouse was empty. There was little light, but there was enough to show him that much.

So where . . .

Somewhere nearby there was a flash of bright yellow light and the sharp report of a pistol being fired.

Longarm caught a glimpse of the muzzle flash to his right and at almost the same moment heard the thump of a lead slug boring into the pine wall of the outhouse.

Instinctively he ducked and leaped forward, into the close confinement of the outhouse.

He hadn't any more than gotten inside before he realized it was a mistake.

From inside the two-holer he could not fight back, while Jimmy Jay could stand outside and pepper the shitter with lead until Longarm was down and done for. There was nowhere in there to hide, and the walls were much too thin to stop a large-caliber bullet.

"Damn you, Jimmy," he roared.

He heard a peal of laughter in return. "Did you think I wouldn't see you standing right there beside me, Long? Hell, I spotted you in the mirror before you ever reached the bar. Knew it was you right off. How you been, Marshal? Still losing at cards?"

"We need to talk, Jimmy," Longarm shouted. "There's something I need to tell you."

"Nothing I'd be interested in hearing," Jay called back.

"I'm serious, Jimmy. Help me out here, and I'll talk to the U.S. attorney about maybe getting you a pardon."

"You lie, Long."

"No, I'm not, Jimmy. You know my word is good."

"I've heard that, yes."

"So what d'you have to lose? Let's talk."

"All right. Throw your gun out and step out with your hands high."

"All right. Give me a minute here."

"You got no time, Long. Come out now or I'll turn that crapper into a sieve."

"Don't be in a rush, Jimmy. I'm coming. I just . . . I got to get my nerve up a little before I toss my gun out, that's all."

"Hurry up, Long. I'm fixing to start the fireworks."

Longarm stepped as far back from the door as he could, dropped down into a low crouch . . . and threw himself at the spring-loaded outhouse door.

Chapter 17

The door burst open so hard the top hinge broke, and the heavy door sagged drunkenly off the one remaining hinge.

Longarm hit the ground and rolled, trying to throw Jimmy Jay's aim off. He expected another gunshot. Another attempt on his life. Instead he heard only laughter.

"Shit, Long, now you went and got that nice new suit dirty. Be careful you don't dent that derby, Long. It's handsome."

Longarm had a good idea of where Jimmy Jay was but not good enough to shoot at. He was somewhere to the left, standing in deep shadow, damn him. There was a shed over there and a small stable. Likely he was inside one of them. But which one?

"What are you doing here, Long? Dressed up like that and traveling with that cheap gambler and a pair of doxies? You're up to something, Long. Want to tell me about it?"

"Sure. That's what I want to sit down and talk to you about," Longarm called back to him.

The shed. Longarm was almost certain Jimmy Jay was in the shed. Or maybe standing right beside it.

Or maybe not.

Damn it anyway!

Longarm would almost welcome another gunshot. At least that would pinpoint Jimmy Jay's location for him so he could shoot back.

"I don't mind telling you what I'm here for, Long. I came to meet a man that wanted to hire me. No idea who he wanted shot. A federal judge maybe. That's what I was hoping for, anyhow. I mean, now that you bastards are already after me, what have I got to lose? Used to be different, you know. I was real careful about who I got mad. Then the stinking son of a bitch asshole federal judges trumped up that postmaster charge against me. That's bullshit, and you know it. I was after a stagecoach man, not a damn post office clerk.

"Now there's nothing to hold me back. Did you ever think about that, Long? Did you? Now I can kill deputies. Judges. Even United States attorneys. It won't get me in any deeper than I already am. They should've thought about that before they rigged those charges against me. What do you say to that, Long? Huh?"

"I already told you, Jimmy. The two of us need to sit down and talk. It could be that I can get the U.S. attorney in Denver to drop those charges. Or get one of the judges to give you a pardon. That way you'd be back where you used to be, with only state and territorial courts looking for you. Us federals would be out of the picture again."

"I don't think you can do that, Long."

"I do, Jimmy. I really do."

"Why would you do that for me, Long?"

"Because I need your help, that's why. I got something going here, but I'm not sure I can do it alone. I could use the help of somebody who knows his way around in, let's say, circles I don't generally run in."

"I still think you're lying, Long."

Which in fact Longarm was. What he hoped—apart from convincing Jimmy that he oughtn't to shoot deputy

U.S. marshal Custis Long—was to get Jimmy Jay safely locked up. Then the various states and territories where the man was wanted could divide the carcass and gnaw on the bones however they pleased.

If that happened, why, Longarm would be delighted to talk to the U.S. attorney about dropping the federal charges against Jimmy. After all, the federal government did not hang anyone, not for anything other than treason or a soldier's desertion in the face of an enemy. There were no capital offenses in the normal course of federal law.

The states, on the other hand, could execute for any number of offenses, nearly all of which Jimmy Jay had committed many times over.

The worst that could happen to Jimmy in federal custody was a long prison sentence. In almost any state west of the Mississippi, and some east of it, too, Jimmy's penalty would be a short rope.

"What do you say, Jimmy? Can we sit down and talk? We sat down together at the card table that time. I'd like to do it again."

"A week ago I might've gone for it, Long. But not now. I can't."

"I don't understand, Jimmy."

"I guess you haven't heard, then."

"Obviously not," Longarm called, still trying to see. He thought he saw some movement just to the right of the shed. Was that Jimmy? Dammit, he wasn't sure.

One properly aimed shot at a target he was sure of and this whole situation would be resolved. And Jimmy Jay would no longer be of interest to anyone except the undertaker in Hyde's Junction.

"I was up in Montana last week, Long."

"Yes. So what?"

"Do you remember a deputy name of Bob Herndon?

73

Robert D., I think the newspaper up there said his proper name was."

"Sure, I know him. Bob's a good man."

"Was, maybe. Not now."

"You killed Bob?"

"He tried to take me, Long. I couldn't allow that. So I put a bullet in his belly. Then put another in his head to make sure he didn't suffer. You could say it was the humanitarian thing to do."

"Damn you, Jimmy!"

"Point is, Long, I don't think they're going to let something like that go. So, sorry, we won't be having that little talk. I'll tell you what, though. The man I'm here to see hasn't showed up yet, and I don't have anything better to do until he gets here. So I think I'm going to spend a day or two hunting. You know what I'm going to be hunting, Long? Or who?"

"I think maybe I do, Jimmy."

"Yeah. I'll just bet you do, Long. Could happen at any time. Any place. You'll never suspect it until it's too late."

"Jimmy."

"Yes, Long?"

"Bob Herndon was a good man. But I'm better." Longarm was almost positive he had Jimmy spotted now. He flattened himself against the ground and took careful aim. If he could just get the SOB to fire one more shot to mark the exact spot, Longarm knew he would have him.

"Good night, Long."

Longarm heard the crunch of gravel under a boot. And then nothing.

Jimmy Jay seemed to have left.

And the shadow Longarm had been focused on, thinking he was looking at Jimmy, was still there. Jesus!

The night air was cool, but Longarm was sweating when he finally stood upright and brushed himself off.

Longarm was playing a cat and mouse game with this Leo Batson. But now it seemed that J. Jimmy Jay was playing one of his own. And Custis Long was the mouse, dammit.

Chapter 18

Just about anywhere else, Longarm thought, a string of
gunshots in the back yard would have drawn attention.
Lots of it. Town marshals and curious bystanders and God
knew what-all else. Not in Hyde's Junction. Here the
night returned to utter silence.

Not a soul so much as looked out to see who, if anyone, was dead after all that.

Longarm brushed himself off as best he could and retrieved the stupid-looking derby, thinking the incident
might have had a positive side to it if it had only resulted
in the loss of that hat. He felt like an idiot, wearing the
thing.

When he went back inside the others were still at the
table where he'd left them.

But then, he realized, he'd only been gone a few
minutes. They probably thought he'd just stepped outside
to take a leak and might not even have heard anything in
here over the buzz of a dozen conversations. Lord knew
what all these crooks were plotting with all the talk.

He got the drinks he'd originally gone to buy and carried them to the table. He briefly explained about J. Jimmy
Jay and their excursion outside, then asked if any of the

77

three knew Jay or knew anything about him.

"No, sorry, I never heard of him," Frankie said. He sounded quite positive about it. But then, Longarm reflected, Frankie would have sounded just as sure even if he were the one who'd summoned Jimmy Jay here to the Hyde Inn.

"From what you tell us, the man is a ruffian," Cherie put in. "Not at all our sort of people."

"You don't know him, then?" Longarm asked.

"Certainly not," Cherie said, managing to sound as if she'd been offended by the idea of her being acquainted with someone like that.

"For what it's worth," Ruby said. "I've at least heard of this Jay before now. I had charge of his girlfriend once. A real slut, that one. She was in for drunk and disorderly, petty larceny, and half a dozen other things. They should have locked her little pink ass away for a while to teach her some respect. Instead, they let her plead to one or two very minor charges and put her on a train. If she ever comes back to Cheyenne she has to serve a ninety-day sentence. Personally I hope she comes back. I'd like to have the little bitch long enough to teach her some manners."

Ruby was looking the other way, but Longarm caught the look Cherie gave Ruby in response to that remark. But then little Cherie had probably spent some time behind bars herself. Her sympathies would all be with Jimmy Jay's girlfriend.

"This isn't getting us anywhere," Longarm said. "Do any of you remember the man I was standing next to at the bar?"

"Not me."

"No."

Ruby merely shrugged and shook her head.

Longarm sighed. "I was hoping you could help me

watch for him. He's here to meet somebody. He won't go far."

"Point him out to us the next time you see him," Cherie suggested. Longarm was sure from her tone of voice that she was quite serious about the idea, too.

Longarm sighed a second time. "Cherie, the next time I see Jimmy Jay, one of us is likely gonna wind up dead. But after I kill the son of a bitch I will let you look him over all you want, I promise."

"I was only tryin' t' be helpful," Cherie pouted.

"He knows that, dear. He's just upset about being shot at tonight," Ruby said, patting the girl's wrist.

"Well I don't know why he's gettin' snippy with me. I didn't shoot at him."

"It might help matters, Long, if you let me have some powder and ball for my pistol," Frankie offered. "I could, like, watch your back."

"Or shoot me in the back," Longarm said.

"Please! We're all friends here, aren't we?"

"No, Frankie, we are not all friends here, so don't think I've forgotten the way you looked back in Denver holding that gun on me."

"That was before we became acquainted, Long. Don't be so touchy."

Longarm rolled his eyes.

"Mr. Long . . . I mean, Mr. Smith," Cherie said with a phony smile, "could I please have another champagne cocktail?"

What the hell, Longarm thought. She was only trying to lighten the mood. And take a little of the heat away from her lad, Frankie. "Sure, Cherie, I'll get you one. Anybody else want a refill? Ruby, d'you want to change your mind and have something to drink?"

The big gal gave him a prissy look, lips so tight together that a white line showed around them. "Not for me, thank you."

"I'd have another," Frankie said.

Longarm figured he could stand another, too. At the government's expense.

He stood and returned to the bar. This time there was no one there who seemed interested in shooting him.

Chapter 19

Longarm tapped the call bell on the counter in the lobby and a moment later the hotel owner, Ben Sanders, emerged from his little office, a book in one hand and a pair of Ben Franklin half-glasses perched on the bridge of his nose. Despite the book and glasses he looked like he had been dozing.

"Sorry to disturb you," Longarm said, "but I have a question, if you don't mind."

"That depends on the question," Sanders said.

"A little while ago I was talking with a fellow in the bar over there. I don't find him now, and I'd like to continue our conversation." Longarm smiled. "He seemed a congenial fellow. And I've thought of a few more points to support the position I was taking.

"He's about this tall—" Longarm held his hand out, palm downward, to indicate someone of slightly less than medium height, "—with sandy hair, blue eyes, medium build, and real shaggy eyebrows. I didn't catch his name."

"That sounds like it would be Mr. Berry. Checked in this afternoon."

"Is he one of your regulars?" Longarm inquired.

"As it happens, he is not. Why would you ask something like that, Mr. Smith?" Sanders did not sound pleased.

Longarm flashed another smile. "Sorry. I'm just a curious sort o' fella, I guess. Didn't mean t' be rude."

"Not at all."

"Could I get away with one more question, please?"

"That depends on the question, Mr. Smith."

"Like I said, I'd like t' buy the gentleman a drink or two an' continue our conversation. Could I ask what room he's in?"

Sanders paused for a moment, then shrugged. "Third floor. Number twenty-seven."

"Is he in?"

"As far as I know, yes. He hasn't left his key at the desk."

"All right, thanks."

"Certainly." Sanders still seemed uncertain about being so free with someone else's information. Probably, Longarm thought, it was a very good thing the innkeeper wanted to have that three way frolic with Cherie and Ruby. He would not want to piss off Ruby's pimp, and that was almost certainly what he would think Longarm was.

Longarm went back into the hotel saloon and got the others. "Bedtime," he told them.

"What? It's still early. We have to be seen, you know. Have to visit with our friends," Frankie said.

Longarm gave him a long, level look but did not say a word.

"All right," Frankie said. "I suppose we could go up now."

The four of them went upstairs to their rooms, all entering the one Longarm and Frankie had taken.

"There's something I have to do," Longarm said, "and I don't want you two—" he looked back and forth between Frankie and Cherie, "—out where you can get yourselves in trouble. Be easier for Ruby to keep an eye on you in here.

"Keep them together, Ruby, where you can see them both. You can handle them by yourself if you have to?"

She gave Longarm a dirty look.

"No offense," he said. "Anybody have to go to take a leak or anything? Once I leave there won't be any privacy for any o' the three of you until I get back. None at all. Understood?"

"I better go, myself," Ruby said. She disappeared into the adjoining room.

"I'll go, too," Cherie said and followed.

"This may be your last chance for a while," Longarm told Frankie.

"No need, thanks."

"Suit yourself."

When the women returned, Longarm told Ruby, "If they try anything, shoot them. An' it's up to you, but my advice would be if you have to shoot one then you'd best go ahead an' shoot the other one, too, otherwise you're apt to end up with a mess on your hands an' we don't want that."

"Very well," Ruby said. She motioned Frankie and Cherie to the side of Longarm's bed, then perched on the forward edge of the one chair in the room. Her posture was primly erect. From somewhere, so smoothly that Longarm did not even see where, she produced a short but rather large-caliber nickel-plated revolver, which she held in her lap. "Don't worry about a thing," she told Longarm. "I'm sure we will have no problems."

Cherie did not seem overly concerned, but Frankie eyed Ruby's pistol with obvious trepidation.

The lovebirds, Longarm thought, were in good hands with Ruby Bradbury.

He let himself out and used his key to lock the door behind him, then headed for the stairs.

Room twenty-seven, the gent downstairs had said.

Chapter 20

The gentleman in room twenty-seven was not, as they say, in residence at the moment.

Longarm picked the lock to let himself in, then located the bedside lamp and lit it.

The room was tidy. Jimmy Jay's things were just as he had left them, including a rope ladder piled on the floor beside the third-story window, ready for a quick and unexpected escape should it prove necessary. A very thoughtful man, this Jimmy Jay, Longarm thought. A man who obviously believed in planning ahead.

Longarm rummaged through Jay's handsome leather traveling bag, hoping to find something that would help pinpoint who Jimmy Jay really was or where he lived when he was not working.

It was just as well that he did not expect anything because nothing was precisely what he found. Oh, there were clothes, shaving gear, all that usual sort of thing. But nothing that would tell Longarm anything about Jimmy Jay the man, nothing that would indicate who Jay came here to see. Or to kill. It had not escaped Longarm's attention that just because Jay *said* he was here to meet somebody, that that information necessarily had to be true.

85

It would not be beyond reason to think that an assassin might lie to a peace officer.

The only pieces of paper in the room were the sheets of foolscap provided by the hotel for use in conjunction with the thunder mug, and the sheets bound into the three books of poetry that Jay carried with him. Jimmy Jay, the dedicated killer, was a reader of light poetry. Who the hell woulda thought it?

In a small valise Longarm found fifteen rounds of completed ammunition, twenty empty brass cartridge cases, plus a bullet mold, nutcracker loading tool, powder, bullets, and primers. The cases were marked .50–110–550 but Longarm did not think the bullets were quite that big. The cases could well have been necked down to a smaller size to fit Jimmy Jay's rifle.

And thinking of which . . .

The weapon was hidden in the bed beneath the mattress. It took Longarm a little while to find it because the hard leather carrying case was positioned in the exact middle of the bed, where it would not be found in a cursory examination by someone running his hand under the sides of the mattress.

The rifle was plain. Beautiful in its simplicity of design and purpose. There was a custom barrel with no maker's stamp on it mounted in one of the heavy Sharps actions. The buttstock and forearm were of unadorned walnut, no carving, not even checkering cut into the wood. But the wood itself had perfect grain, tight and even. The stock, too, was very much a custom piece, with a high comb to accommodate the sights, which were telescopic.

The telescope tube was dark so the metal would not reflect sunlight too readily, although a few very small bright scratch marks suggested it was made of brass beneath that finish. The rear mount was fitted with knobs and screws that would shift that end of the telescope tube up and down or from side to side, so as to adjust the aiming point.

Longarm held the rifle to his shoulder. It was a heavy son of a bitch, but very comfortable, and with its long, exceptionally heavy barrel was easy to hold steady.

Thin black lines were visible through the glass magnification of the telescope. Crosshairs, he believed those were called by the people who favored such things as these optical sights. The sights were too delicate and unreliable for his taste. A hard jar would knock them out of alignment, and a rain or even a very humid day could make them fog over and become impossible to use. Other than the crosshairs all he could see through the tube right now was a blue of light and dark. Objects would have to be far away in order to be seen clearly through the telescope, much farther than the very limited space within the hotel room walls.

Such devices were much too fragile and unreliable for Longarm's taste. He doubted they would ever catch on, except perhaps with competitive target-shooters.

Or someone in Jimmy Jay's line of work, who would certainly find them useful. The magnifying sights would allow him to kill from very long range and have plenty of time to melt away before anyone might discover where his shot came from.

And if the day were not suitable for the use of the device, if it was foggy, say, or too windy, Jimmy Jay could simply wait for a better time to do his hired murder.

Longarm shuddered once and wondered how many men this rifle had killed. And probably every single one of them a person of more genuine worth than the man who'd killed them.

On an impulse, Longarm held the beautiful rifle by the muzzle and with a grunt of effort slammed it down onto the iron footboard of the hotel room bed. He smashed the telescope first, destroying it with that first swing, then struck out several more times to break the hammer and then the trigger guard and trigger.

The rifle could be repaired, of course, by any competent gunsmith. But no son of a bitch could pick it up right now and use it to murder another innocent soul.

Longarm took the now broken rifle with him when he returned to their rooms on the floor below. He left everything else there, but with no effort to hide the fact that he had fingered through everything.

If Jimmy Jay should happen to return to this room, Longarm wanted the SOB to know he'd been there. Just to piss him off.

Angry men, after all, tend to make mistakes.

Chapter 21

Longarm did not believe he had ever seen anyone angrier—or more frustrated—than Ruby Bradbury was. But then she did have a pretty good reason to be upset.

When Longarm walked into the hotel room he was sharing with Frankie Powell, there was no sign of Ruby, Frankie, and Cherie. All three were in the adjoining room.

And even Longarm was startled by what he found there.

Ruby was seething, so furious she was close to tears.

Frankie was lying naked on top of the bed in that room.

And Cherie, also naked, was kneeling between Frankie's legs with her round, pink little ass in the air and the scrawny gambler's cock in her mouth. Cherie was rather noisily slurping and sucking away.

"They . . . they . . . I couldn't . . . they just . . . ," Ruby sputtered helplessly. "I didn't know . . . I just don't think . . ."

The big matron began to cry.

Longarm patted her shoulder and wondered if a hug would help calm her down. Probably not, he decided. She would just think he was trying to get some of what Frankie was having and become even unhappier.

89

"It's all right," he said. "Don't let them get to you."

Frankie looked at Longarm and grinned.

Cherie remained oblivious to everything except her concentration on Frankie's rigid and wetly glistening pecker.

Longarm took the few strides necessary to cross the room. He took Cherie by the hair and lifted her off Frankie.

"Hey!" Frankie yelped in protest. "I ain't done yet."

"Trust me. You're done," Longarm said.

"No, he needs this. He really does," Cherie said. "He gets all grouchy and out of sorts if he can't get off. It isn't good for his health, neither."

"Who told you that? Him?"

The girl wiped her mouth with the back of her hand and nodded. She continued to hold Frankie's balls in her other hand. "I can do you next if you want me to."

Longarm sighed. "You're embarrassing Miss Bradbury."

Cherie giggled. Frankie grinned some more. The gambler looked proud of himself.

He had known, of course, that Ruby would not shoot him. Not for something like this. And while he probably did want a blow job from Cherie—who the hell wouldn't—it probably pleased him every bit as much to be able to yank Ruby around.

"Cherie, put your clothes on."

"What about me, Long?" Frankie asked. "Do I hafta get dressed, too?" His voice was thick with smart-ass insolence.

"No, Frankie, you're free to do whatever you please. But then, so am I." Longarm picked Cherie up and set her aside, managing to do it without any visible sign of effort. But then she was not a very big girl.

Frankie's smug grin disappeared when Longarm took a handful of his hair and flung him off the bed.

The gambler hit the floor with a thump. He let out a squawk and rolled, but not quickly enough to avoid the toe of Longarm's boot, which caught him high on his hip and landed hard.

"Hey! Jesus. Don't do tha . . ."

Longarm kicked him again. In his hairy ass this time. Frankie began scampering on hands and knees for the connecting door into the other bedroom.

"My apologies," Longarm said to Ruby. He tipped his hat to her, then followed Frankie, catching up with the gambler in time to give him another boot in the butt before he cleared the doorway.

Very gently Longarm pulled the door closed behind him, and stood over a cowering and trembling Frankie.

"You didn't hafta do that," Frankie grumbled, rubbing his hip. A red spot had appeared there where Longarm's boot connected. "You treated me like I'm some kinda cur dog."

"Now, Frankie, you are wrong about that," Longarm said, taking out a cheroot and nipping the twist off with his teeth. "I wouldn't kick a dumb animal like a dog. It wouldn't be respectful. But I'll kick the shit out of any son of a bitch who acts like an animal." He dipped two fingers into his vest pocket and produced a match, which he used to light the cheroot. "Am I making myself clear here, Frankie?"

"Yeah."

Longarm's expression hardened. "What?"

"I said yes, dammit."

"*What*?" Longarm roared.

"Yes, sir!" Frankie barked, his eyes wide and fearful.

"Where're your clothes?"

Frankie pointed mutely toward the closed door into the other room.

Longarm tapped on the door, which Ruby opened a moment later. She was already holding Frankie's clothes, and apparently had intended to return them even before Longarm knocked.

"I'm sorry," she said in a very small voice. "I should have . . . I didn't know what to do. He just . . . ordered her. And took off his . . . his things. He didn't care that I was watching. Didn't care at all. I should have done . . . I don't know what. I should have done something."

"You should have kicked him in the balls, is what you should have done," Longarm said.

Ruby blushed, her face and neck flushing a dull, burning red.

"You aren't used to handling men, are you?"

Ruby shook her head. "I'm sorry."

"Don't be. But next time, and there very likely will be a next time, although God knows what he will do to try and push you around the next time, next time, Ruby, you should beat the crap outa him. Or her."

"I know how to handle women. That may be hard for you to believe, Marshal, but I am a very good matron. I can control the women in my charge. It is just . . . I never imagined . . . I mean, I never. Really."

Longarm smiled a little. "Yeah. Who the hell would've thought it."

Ruby shuddered. Then she too smiled. Just a little. "I will certainly have something to tell all the other girls in the boarding house when I get back to Cheyenne, won't I?"

"Yes, you certainly will. Are you all right now, d'you think?"

"I'm fine. Thank you."

"If you need anything, any help or anything at all . . ."

"I won't," Ruby assured him. "I can take care of Cherie just fine, I promise you."

"I know you can," Longarm said, although the truth was that he was no longer sure if he believed that himself.

Not that he wanted Ruby to know that he was having doubts about her. But he was.

Ruby was right. She *should* have done something when Frankie decided to show off like that.

Still, Longarm had more pressing matters than Frankie Powell's sex life to worry about right now. Like J. Jimmy Jay. Jay was out there somewhere. Without his rifle, true, but rifles can be replaced, and all it would take would be one well aimed shot from ambush and Longarm's whole day would be fucked up.

"Good night, Ruby."

"Good night, Marshal."

Longarm closed the connecting door and dumped Frankie's clothes unceremoniously onto the floor beside it.

Frankie began to rise, but Longarm stopped him with a hard look and a warning gesture. "Stay right there, asshole."

"But my clothes . . ."

"You can have them in the morning. You want naked? I'll give you naked, mister. Now hold your hands out. Right hand first. If you want to try anything with me, feel free."

Frankie went pale. And held his hands out one at a time, so Longarm could handcuff him to the metal bed frame.

"I need a blanket. And you said I could sleep on a pallet. I need something to sleep on," Frankie whined.

"If you don't shut the fuck up, mister, I'll put you to sleep with a boot upside your ugly head. Now be quiet."

"I have to take a leak."

"You can reach the thunder mug. Hook it with your foot and drag it over to you."

"But I can't hold it."

"Fine. Get over top of it like you're humping the thing. Or piss on yourself. I really don't care. But whatever you do, bub, you'd best be damn quiet about it because if I

93

hear another word outa you I am gonna stuff a gag in your mouth. D'you understand me, mister?"

"Yes, sir."

"Good. Now lay down an' be quiet. I'm going to bed."

Chapter 22

In the morning Longarm took the cuffs off a very un-happy—but very meek and respectful—Frankie Powell, and let the gambler get dressed. Then he tapped on the connecting door and brought the ladies into the room.

"I have some things to do today. I need to see if I can find Jimmy Jay or figure out what he's up to here. I want you three to stay in the room. We'll go downstairs to socialize and look for this Leo friend of yours later. I'll have breakfast sent up and plan on coming back by lunch-time. We can all go down then. In the meantime, Frankie, I'm going to chain you to that bed again."

"But . . ."

"Don't give me any of your shit, Powell, or I promise I'll give it back ten times over. D'you understand me?"

Frankie did not look happy, but he managed a nod.

"As for you, Cherie, you will do exactly what Miss Bradbury tells you. And you will do nothing but what she tells you. I want you and your pet idiot here to understand something. It is up to me whether we continue this non-sense, and I am about this close—" he pinched his fingers together, "—to loading everybody on a train and heading back to Denver. If I decide to do that, you two are going behind bars for the next couple years. Probably a good many years, once we tell the judge you engaged in fraud, lying to a peace officer, and attempted escape by way of deception. Believe me, I can make a judge think you are a greater menace to society than five mail bombers. And I will do it, too, if you both don't settle down and behave. Am I clear on this? Really good and clear?"

He waited until both of them nodded, Cherie immediately and Frankie reluctantly.

"Now go sit on the foot of the bed," Longarm told Frankie, "and think about which wrist you want cuffed to that footboard. I'll leave one hand free so you can eat or wipe yourself." He turned to Ruby. "If Powell gives you any trouble, ignore him. We'll all take the next train back to Denver if he does."

Longarm got his hat. "Lock this door behind me. I'll have them bring something up for you to eat."

He went downstairs and stopped at the desk to arrange for a large breakfast tray and paid for it, then went outside to find his own morning meal. Not that he expected there would be anything wrong with the Hyde Inn's food. But he did not really expect to see Jimmy Jay seated there with a bowl of porridge or a stack of hotcakes, and while the odds of encountering the assassin on the street or in a café might be slim, they were better than the chance of finding him inside the hotel this morning.

Jimmy Jay's presence in Hydes Junction was unsettling so far as this assignment was concerned. And it did nothing for Longarm's mood to know that the skilled and very efficient killer was out there somewhere, very likely with a mad on for one Custis Long.

Longarm would welcome a showdown with the son of a bitch, and the quicker the better.

Chapter 23

Longarm found a café where they served decent food and excellent coffee. He managed to get a seat where his back would be protected by a wall, while, at the same time, he could keep an eye on the street. He took his time eating breakfast and lingered over coffee, mildly hoping he might spot Jimmy Jay. He had no real expectation of that, though, and was not overly disappointed when the man failed to blunder into Longarm's hands.

When he paid for his meal, he asked, "Where could a man buy a rifle around here?"

"There's a store on the next block. Callan's Hardware. He carries a big stock o' guns. Might have what you're looking for."

"All right, thanks."

Callan's was easy enough to find. It had a sign on the false front that said GUNS in letters four feet tall. The business name was painted much more modestly. Longarm strode inside and took a look around.

The store sold hardware, all right, but the entire back wall and two glass front counters were devoted to fire-arms.

Callan's merchandise was a mighty interesting lot and

reflected the sort of clientele he must get in a town like this. Nearly all the handguns were very small, for instance. Derringers, pocket pistols, sleeve guns, muff guns, even some of the odd-looking knuckle dusters that were as good as useless at any range beyond arm's length.

There were a very few ordinary revolvers, Colts and Remingtons and some Smith and Wessons, but those were in the minority.

In a rack behind the display cases were the long guns. Those, too, were not the ordinary run of Winchesters, Marlins, and Kennedys. They generally fell into one of two distinct categories. The rifles were mostly single-shot weapons of very large caliber, with exceptionally long barrels—Sharps and a few Martinis—while the shotguns were stubby little things, with the double barrels chopped down ridiculously short. A scattergun like that would be of no use at all for hunting, but was just the thing for hiding under a coat or duster.

Funny sort of inventory, Longarm thought. But then, this was a funny sort of town.

"Can I help you, sir?"

"Yes, I . . ." Longarm remembered only after his mouth was already in motion that as far as Hyde's Junction was concerned, he was not Custis Long, United States deputy marshal. He was good ol' Henry Smith, exact occupation unsavory and unstated. Damn it! "Yes, I . . . um . . . I'd like to see one of those rifles. A Sharps, I think."

Callan—at least Longarm assumed the gentleman was the proprietor—smiled. "Do you have a choice of caliber? I have them in sizes ranging from .40 caliber bottleneck cartridges to the old-fashioned .56 straight-wall case."

"I don't know all that much about them, myself," Longarm said. "I'm looking for something that would be accurate at a long distance."

"Then I would recommend something like, uh—" he turned and peered at the rifles on his rack, "—perhaps

98

like this." He took down a Sharps with a case-hardened action, a heavy octagon barrel, and very pretty grain in the highly polished buttstock and forearm.

"This rifle is a .45–90. I can get it for you in .40 or .50 caliber, also, and with case capacities from 60 to 120 grains of powder. You can also have your choice of standard trigger like this one or double-set triggers. If you want me to order in something in particular, I can send a wire off to my distributor today and have your rifle here usually within five days."

"That's good service," Longarm said. He accepted the very heavy weapon from Callan and dropped the underlever to open the action, checked to make sure the rifle was empty, then raised it to his shoulder. "There are no sights," he said.

"The sights are sold separately. I would, of course, be glad to mount them for you free of charge."

Longarm nodded. "Do you have any of those . . . what d'you call them . . . you know, the telescope aiming things."

"You mean telescopic sights."

"Yes, I think so. Do you have any of those?"

"No, they are not popular. It would be foolish to stock them. I can special order one for you if you like, but to tell you the truth I don't know who you could find to mount it for you. I wouldn't attempt a job like that myself. Wouldn't recommend sights like that to you either, friend. They aren't reliable. They are easily jarred out of alignment, and they tend to build up moisture inside the tubes, then they fog up and you can't see through them. Besides, those are for expert riflemen, which you suggest you are not."

"No, I'm not," Longarm said.

"Then I really think you should stick with the regular sights."

"Yes, I'm sure you're right. Do you sell many of those . . . what did you call them again?"

"The telescopic sights?"

"Yes, that was it. Do you sell very many of them?"

"To tell you the truth, sir, I've never sold one in my life."

"How about these long-barreled rifles. Is there much call for them?" Longarm asked.

"I sell one every now and then. Otherwise, it would make no sense for me to stock them. I would not say that I sell a great many, though. Most of my trade in firearms is in those pistols." Callan smiled. "Although I see you are not likely to be interested in any of them. Unless you want something to back up that . . . is that one of the Colt double-action revolvers you are carrying?"

"Yes, sir. And you're right. I wouldn't be interested in any of the little derringers." Longarm did not mention the fact that he also had one of those, a custom made brass frame .41 that resided in his vest pocket at the end of his watch chain.

"Would you like for me to mount a set of sights on this rifle for you? I could have it done by this afternoon."

"That's mighty nice of you, Mr. Callan, but I'd best think this over before I decide. Like I told you, I don't know all that much about such things. Is there, um, is there anyone around who maybe could teach me?"

"Naturally, I would share with you whatever knowledge I possess, but . . . let me think . . . I do not know right offhand about anyone locally who would be expert with the long-range rifles."

"Anyone passing through maybe? Any recent customers?" Longarm asked.

Callan shook his head. "No. I'm sorry."

Which did not necessarily mean that Jimmy Jay had not yet found a replacement for his rifle. But it did suggest that.

Longarm found Callan's information to be much more valuable than the storekeeper could possibly have guessed. He smiled. "Thanks for your help. I'll check back with you later. And if you do come across anyone you think might be able to teach me about these things, I'd sure be interested in knowing it. My name is Henry Smith, and I'm staying at the Inn."

"You will let me know about the rifle, then?"

"Yes, sir, and I think if I do get one, you'll have t' order it. I'll come by another time an' let you know what I decide to do."

"Very good, Mr. Smith, and I shall find my catalog so I can go over with you all the options that are available. There is a bewildering number of them. Barrel lengths, and weights, and shapes. Stock sizes and shapes. Calibers. Triggers. Endless variables, you see. Don't worry, though. I will be glad to assist you."

"You're very kind, sir."

"My pleasure, Mr. Smith."

Longarm touched the brim of the silly derby and ambled out of Callan's Hardware.

Chapter 24

He reached into his coat pocket for a cheroot, then grimaced. He'd forgotten to get more of the tasty little cigars out of the supply in his carpetbag. He doubted he could find anything in this small town to compare with the quality of the smokes that were available back home in Denver. That was precisely why he always kept the bag well stocked with his favorites. Someone in Longarm's position could find himself traveling with no advance notice and not have time to stop at the tobacconist's.

Fat lot of good that foresight did him this time.

Resigned to having to make do, he turned up the street toward a mercantile whose sign advertised tobacco along with half a dozen other items, including hats, boots, and ready-to-wear.

Longarm ambled in that direction and mounted the wooden sidewalk. He passed through the open doorway and was immediately greeted by a cheerfully called, "Custis Long! What a sight for sore eyes."

Inwardly Longarm groaned. He was supposed to be Henry damn Smith here. Now who. . . .

"Good morning, Nellie." He swept his hat off. "What an unexpected pleasure to find you here." That was partially true. It was unexpected. It was no pleasure. "And why so early?"

Buttonhook Nellie—she was certain to have a last name, but Longarm had never heard it; for that matter, it was almost as certain that her real first name was not Nellie—came flying across the store and gave Longarm a huge hug. At least, as best she could manage. She was handicapped by the fact that her fat kept her from getting a very good wrap around him.

Buttonhook Nellie took her name from an incident in Wichita during the heyday of the cattle droving industry. Young as she must have been then, Nellie was already the proud proprietress of her own whorehouse. Her place had a reputation for cleanliness and order, and a man could go there secure in the knowledge that his pocket would not be picked while he was busy having his fun.

Nellie took care of her girls as well as her clients, though, and one late night a cowboy from Alabama became rowdy and began beating up his chosen partner. Nellie broke the lock on the door to get inside, and when she saw what the cowboy was doing to her prize doxy, Nellie stopped the assault by killing the sonuvabitch. She did it with the button hook she happened to have in her hand when all the commotion started. Shoved the steel hook into the fellow's eye socket, and stirred it around and around.

It was said the man's family was told he died of unspecified natural causes.

Which Longarm always thought was entirely reasonable. After all, it was perfectly natural for a fellow to die if his brains were scrambled while he happened still to be using them.

Nellie left Wichita years back and moved further west. To Pueblo, to Fountain, then to Colorado City, which was where Longarm knew her from.

Longarm returned the tubby woman's hug, and in a near whisper said, "We got to talk, Nellie."

She disengaged herself from him, and peered up—a considerable distance upward, as she was a good foot and a half shorter than Longarm but probably outweighed him by sixty or seventy pounds—with a speculative look in her eye. "Do you know where my place is, Custis?"

"No, I surely do not."

She gave him directions. "We'll be back there in about an hour."

Over on the far side of the store were half a dozen young women who he now realized must be Nellie's whores, the "we" she just referred to.

"What are . . ."

Nellie gave him an exasperated look. "I know, I know, it's practically the break of day." It was the middle of the morning, but to Nellie that was about as close as she and her companions could come to daybreak. "This is a wonderful town, Custis, but there are a few meddlesome biddies . . . there always have to be some it seems, even here . . . who just can't stand the idea that whores are people, too. They treat their cats better than they want us treated. We don't mind being kept off the streets except for one shopping day a week. We're used to that. But everywhere else I've ever heard of, the shopping time for soiled doves is in the afternoon, for God's sake. Here they set Tuesdays from nine until eleven in the damn morning as the time when we can come out onto their precious streets. Malicious bitches!"

"I'm sorry, Nellie. I really am." More than she could know, he thought to himself.

"I wonder if you could do something about it for us, Custis. Now that you're here . . ."

"Nellie, we really do need to talk. But not here, please. An' not now. An' please quit calling me Custis out so's anybody might hear."

Nellie's eyebrows wiggled up and down, but she wasn't flirting. She was thinking.

"All right, dear. We'll be done here in just a little while. I'll not say anything until after we've had our little chat."

Longarm gave the woman another hug and let her return to her chattering but obviously curious whores. One of them asked something in a voice too low for Longarm to hear. He did catch the words "old friend" in Nellie's answer to the young, bucktoothed blonde girl.

That was all right, then.

Longarm left the whores to their shopping and went to the back of the store.

Whoever did the buying for the place obviously knew quality when it came to cigars, and Longarm ended up buying a fistful of them, instead of the one or two that would have served until he could get back to the hotel to his own supply.

Chapter 25

Longarm had no trouble finding Nellie's current place of business. He simply asked the barber who shaved him where he could find the cleanest whorehouse in town. It turned out there was a scandalously large number of them to choose from—scandalous, that is, for those biddies Nellie spoke of earlier—but the cleanest was a low, rambling, one-story structure set somewhat apart from the others.

Only one floor. No stairs to climb. That had to be Nellie's. Longarm followed the directions the barber gave him and found it with no difficulty.

He kept close to the sides of the buildings he passed, not wanting to make too easy a target of himself, in case Jimmy Jay already found a rifle and was hunting for him. He felt a small chill of apprehension tickling the base of his spine when he left the relative protection of the town and walked the final half block between vacant lots in order to reach the whorehouse.

That son of a bitch Jay had to be someplace. He had to be furious. And he had to be on the prowl, eager to kill Longarm so he could make his connection with that would-be employer.

Longarm reached the front door of the whorehouse without any shots being fired. Nellie must have been watching for him, because she opened it herself just as he was stepping up onto the wide, shallow front porch.

"This way, dear." She led him through the foyer and past an ornately furnished parlor to an office/bedroom suite at one side of the place, adjacent to the kitchen. Apparently the working rooms, which doubled as living quarters for the girls, were all the way on the other end of the structure.

Nellie motioned Longarm to a very comfortable wing-back chair and said, "You won't have to worry about being overheard here, dear. Everyone but me is asleep by now."

"Good," he said. "First thing, Nellie. My name is not Custis Long. I'm Henry Smith. It's important to me."

"Goodness. You haven't come over to our side of the law, have you?" She was smiling when she said it.

"You know better'n that." He took out a pair of cheroots and offered one to Nellie, then lit both of them from a single match. "Besides, Nellie, you aren't a criminal."

"That depends on who you ask, doesn't it?"

"I don't need t' ask anybody about that. I know. You're all right an' always have been."

"Why, thank you, Cu . . . Henry. Coming from you that is a compliment that I value. Thank you very much."

"Just telling a simple truth, that's all."

"Now that you have me properly buttered up," she asked, "what is it you want me to do?"

"D'you know a man name of Jimmy Jay?"

Nellie shook her head. "It doesn't sound familiar."

Longarm described him and added, "He dresses well and acts decent. You wouldn't think it if you met him, but he's an assassin. And good at his work, too. Makes a lot of money and enjoys the finer things that money can buy. He might come here if he's feeling randy."

"If he does pay us a visit, what would you like me to do?"

"Tell whatever girl is with him to find out as much as she can from him. Where he's staying is what I'll most need to know. And quick as him an' the girl are out o' sight, send someone running to fetch me. I'm at the hotel. And under the name Henry Smith, don't forget."

"Is this Jay person the reason why you are here, dear?"

"No, but I had a run-in with Jimmy last night and now he's gunning for me. He likes to shoot from ambush at long range, and I wouldn't much enjoy that."

"If he comes here, would you like for me to kill him for you, dear?"

Nellie's tone of voice and expression were perfectly matter-of-fact. She obviously thought there was nothing at all unusual in the question. Longarm very quickly shook his head. "Good Lord, no. I don't want you involved any more'n you have to be. Besides, it'd be bad for business." He grinned. "I wouldn't want to ruin your reputation."

That brought a belly laugh out of the fat madam. "Custis . . . Henry, I mean . . . I do love you. You know that, don't you?"

"Ah, hell, Nellie, I love you, too."

"Good. Let's fuck."

"Nellie! I didn't mean it that way."

Her expression changed. It lost the lighthearted, laughing quality and became somber. "I'm serious, dear. I really am crazy about you. And I *do* mean it that way. I always have been. Whenever I look at you I get all wet and drippy, and I want to feel you inside me. Do you remember Colorado City, dear?"

"I remember, Nellie. You were mighty good to me. I won't never forget that."

He wouldn't, either. It was before he had signed on to ride as one of Billy Vail's deputies, before he'd become known as Longarm. He was broke at the time and between jobs. He had been sick. Burning up with fever and too weak to walk properly, much less look for work.

Buttonhook Nellie had taken him in and nursed him back to health. When he was well enough to leave, on his last night there, she'd appeared beside his bed, naked and horny, and climbed on top of him. The experience had been . . . memorable. To say the least. Not good. Not for him, anyway. But certainly memorable.

"Do I have to beg for it, Custis? I will, you know. I'll get down on my knees right now and beg you."

"God no, Nellie. Don't do that. Please don't be doin' that."

But damned if she didn't come over before him and drop onto her knees. With one hand she reached for his buttons. And with the other she began undoing her own.

Oh, shit! he thought. How can I get outa this without hurting Nellie's feelings?

Chapter 26

He closed his eyes.

The sight of all that pale, lumpy, sagging, dimpled flesh was about enough to turn a man's stomach and make him swear off sex for a month.

But it wasn't half bad if he just shut his eyes and let the sensations wash over him.

Nellie hadn't come into the profession of running whorehouses simply as a business decision. She'd come up through the ranks, starting out whoring as a young girl and working her way, saving money, studying how other madams and whoremasters conducted themselves.

At a time when most madams extracted sixty percent of their girls' take, Buttonhook Nellie took only a flat fifty percent of the up-front price and let the girls keep anything they got in tips. That quite naturally brought all the best girls into Nellie's stable and made them eager to stay with her. Nellie set the rules, and they were quick to abide by them.

But all of that came later, after Nellie left the active part of the trade in order to enter management.

Along the way she had learned to give one hell of a fine blow job.

Which she demonstrated for Longarm now.

He stood with his britches puddled around his ankles and his balls cupped warm and snug in the palm of Nellie's hand. His dick was socketed deep into Nellie's throat while at the same time she very lightly tickled his asshole with a fingernail. The combination of feelings was better than merely good.

Nellie's tongue worked tirelessly, and she bobbed her head to take him in and out of the wet heat.

With his eyes closed . . .

"Custis darlin', I can't wait any more," she said.

When she released him from her mouth, the air hit his dripping wet pecker and chilled him there.

He opened his eyes. Pretty much had to.

And he regretted it as soon as he'd done it. Nellie hadn't gotten any better looking in the last couple minutes.

She stood and turned around and bent over the side of her desk to present her ass to him. Longarm had seen barn doors smaller than that pink, pimpled spread.

But there was a nest of hair with a wet pussy winking at him out of the middle, and his boner hadn't yet gone down. Not after the build-up Nellie had given it with her mouth. After that he would've been willing and able to screw a longhorn cow.

Or a fat madam.

Nellie whimpered with sheer ecstasy when Longarm shuffled over behind her and shoved his pole in.

Powder River, let 'er buck.

Hot womanflesh surrounded him, and Nellie quivered and cried out.

The hanging folds of flab flowed and jiggled with Longarm's stroking motion.

Oh, hell, he silently moaned.

He closed his eyes and pummeled hard and fast.

Chapter 27

"Custis dear, I do love you. Thank you." Nellie gave him another of her incomplete hugs with her stubby, flabby arms. He didn't shudder. Hell, he liked her. As a friend, that is. *Only* as a friend. Longarm leaned down and gave her a light peck on the forehead.

"If we see anything of this Jay person, dear, I will let you know."

"Right away, please. Just don't put yourself or any o' your girls into danger because of it. But if he does come in, well, I'd like to know about it right away."

"You know I would do anything for you," Nellie said. Could be she even meant it. He gave her a hug and told her good-bye.

When he stepped outside it was coming on toward noon. Lunchtime. He needed to get back to the hotel so he could bring his "guests"—prisoners? snitches? he wasn't exactly sure what they were at this point—downstairs to mingle with the other criminals and ne'er-do-wells staying at the Hyde Inn. That, after all, was his purpose in being here. Leo Batson was the target of this deal. Grabbing J. Jimmy Jay would be good, too, of course. But secondary.

Longarm kept his eyes open on the way back to the Inn, but saw no ambush, no assassin, no trap or danger. No one lurking in alleyways. No gun barrels peeking out of second-story windows. Nothing but horses, ordinary folks, and an occasional stray dog.

That was almost disappointing. He really would have liked to come face to face with Jay one more time, damn him. Jay had won that last round. Longarm could not allow that to happen again.

He reached the hotel without incident and mounted the steps to the porch, took one last, searching look around while he paused at the doorway to light a cheroot, and then stepped inside.

He headed for the staircase leading up to the rooms he shared with Frankie and the women.

"Mr. Smith. Excuse me. Mr. Smith?"

Longarm almost failed to respond to the assumed name. He remembered in time and stopped. "Yes, Mr. Sanders?"

"I have a message for you, sir."

Longarm frowned. He had told them quite clearly, dammit, that all three of them were supposed to stay in that one room. They weren't to go anywhere. Weren't to do anything. Weren't to budge until he got back. So what the hell were they doing leaving a note at the desk?

Damn people who could not understand simple instructions, he silently grumbled even while he crossed the lobby with a relaxed smile on his face. "Thank you, Mr. Sanders."

He accepted an envelope from the chubby hotel keeper—an image flashed through his mind and he damn near burst out laughing; he could just imagine roly-poly Ben Sanders naked and getting it on with blubbery, rubbery Buttonhook Nellie; now wouldn't that be something to see—and smiled his thanks, the smile concealing the merriment Longarm felt at that unexpected picture in his mind's eye. Be a helluva show, though. You could sell tickets. Watch an elephant get it on with a whale. Yes, sir. Helluva show.

Longarm carried the envelope over to the side of the lobby as if for better light to see by, although the truth was that he did not want anyone passing by to get a glimpse of whatever might be in there.

The envelope was sealed with some sort of paste, and he had to tear it to get it open.

There was a single sheet of paper folded over and placed inside.

"I intended only to protect my business interest. You broke my favorite rifle. Now it is personal. Now I think you will die in much pain. Bastard."

The note was signed with the letter J.

And that was more than was really necessary.

The son of a bitch was cheeky enough to come back to the hotel and go to his room, even knowing that Longarm was onto him here.

That was mighty confident of him.

Or very foolishly rash.

Longarm was not sure which of those was true. Perhaps both.

Regardless, Jimmy Jay was one formidable opponent, with or without his favorite rifle in hand.

Longarm was in a deeply pensive mood as he mounted the stairs to their rooms on the second floor.

Chapter 28

Anyone not in the know would have thought Ruby and the two . . . what should he call them, detainees perhaps . . . would have thought they were all in lockup for the past six months at the very least, instead of the past few hours.

Cherie fluttered and preened like a pigeon having a dust bath as she arranged each curl just exactly to her liking, and painted some sort of red shit on her lips, and did something else to darken her eyelashes and the rims around her eyes.

Frankie must have re-tied his necktie half a dozen times and cleaned his shoes with a damp cloth. The same cloth he then decided to rub over his clothes to get any lint off them. The effect was spoiled because he hadn't been able to go to the barber's for a shave and so looked even seedier than usual.

Even Ruby seemed somewhat afflicted with the excitement of being released from confinement. She enlisted Cherie's help to make sure the hem of her dress was hanging properly and that nothing was showing except what ought to.

Longarm just looked at the three of them and marveled at the whole thing.

In the fullness of time—which was pretty damn full, considering how long it took the two women to get ready for the trip downstairs—Longarm led them down to the dining room.

There were several new faces there today, people who had just arrived or perhaps simply had not chosen to socialize last night. Longarm gave Frankie a surreptitious glance and a raising of his eyebrows. He got a nearly imperceptible shake of the head in return. Leo Batson was not among these newcomers. Unfortunately.

It would have pleased Longarm greatly to make his arrest of Batson and immediately get the hell out of Hyde's Junction. Call it running away if you like, but there was simply too much open ground around this little town, ground where Jimmy Jay could lay in wait for Longarm to come under his rifle sights. Longarm would far rather tackle the man on narrowly confined city streets, where an ambush from long range was difficult if not impossible. Longarm wanted to find and to face the man. But on his own terms, thank you, not Jimmy Jay's.

That was not, however, going to happen over lunch in the dining room of the Hyde Inn.

The two women put their heads close together, whispering and giggling over God knew what—the two of them did seem to be getting along quite famously today, despite the displays of anger last night when Cherie was servicing Frankie and Ruby did not know what the hell to do about it—while the estimable Mr. Powell tried to make himself look important and prosperous here among his fellow thieves, mountebanks, charlatans, and scoundrels.

About all he needed to complete this mess now, Longarm reflected, would be an elephant and some circus clowns. Those, he thought, should fit right in.

With a sigh he applied his attention to the menu offerings for the day.

Chapter 29

"Look, I know this isn't exactly what we planned, and I know you don't like being stuck in a hotel room all the time. I just don't have any choice right now. I have to get this thing with Jimmy Jay resolved before the man puts a bullet into my back. So I'm asking you to go back upstairs and wait there until I come back for you."

"Wait a minute," Frankie protested.

Longarm gave him a very cold glare.

"No . . . I . . . it ain't what you think. It's just . . . I got to, well, you know. I can't have Miz Bradbury looking on while I do that."

Longarm relented. The man did have a point. "All right. Ruby, take Cherie and go up to your room. I'll go out back with Frankie so's he can take care of that little problem, then I'll bring him up to join you. And if you're gonna need, uh, relief your own self you'd best do it now. Could be until suppertime before I get back here."

He could see that Ruby did not care for this any more than Frankie and Cherie did, but the matron from Cheyenne nodded.

Longarm paid for their meal and pulled the chair away from the table for Ruby. Frankie let Cherie manage without any assistance from him. The women headed for the staircase while Longarm and Frankie went out the back door.

The back of the hotel in daylight was a cluttered shambles of trash and cast-off bits of broken furniture and housewares. Longarm was amazed that Jimmy Jay had been able to pass through it last night without stumbling or at least giving himself away with a great deal of noise. The man must have eyes like a cat, Longarm thought, to be able to negotiate a mess like this in silence.

"I'm gonna be a minute," Frankie said as he pulled the outhouse door open. "I gotta take a shit."

"Damn, Frankie, that is more information than I really wanted to have, if you don't mind."

"Sorry." The seedy gambler pulled the door closed behind him. A moment later Longarm heard him whistling a light tune.

Longarm leaned against the front of the rough-hewn wood of the outhouse and reached for a cheroot. He nipped the tip off between his teeth and spat out the twist, then fished a match from his vest pocket and scratched it alight, bending his head to the flame.

A flicker of motion in his peripheral vision caught Longarm's attention, and he dropped into a crouch.

Half a block away a rifle barked, and half an instant later a lead slug sizzled over Longarm's head.

If he still had been standing upright . . .

The Colt that came instantly into his hand answered Jay's bullet with one of its own, even though all Longarm had to aim by was a wisp of pale gun smoke beside a broken barrel.

He heard his slug strike. From the sound of it he'd hit wood, though, not flesh.

Longarm cocked the Colt this time, for the lighter trigger pull and better accuracy than if he were pulling the

122

trigger double-action, then waited for Jimmy Jay to show himself.

He waited for what seemed a very long time. Then waited still longer.

Once again there was no rush from the guests inside the Hyde Inn nor from the townspeople to come see what the shooting had been about. Longarm wondered if there was even such a thing as a police chief or town marshal here. If there was, then the man was certainly good at staying clear of other people's troubles.

Eventually—and somewhat reluctantly—Longarm concluded that Jimmy Jay must have taken his shot and then scampered. Or so Longarm hoped, anyway.

Longarm stood upright and, eyes open for any new hint of trouble, reloaded his revolver before he did anything else. Then he tapped away the ash that was hanging on the tip of his cheroot. Finally he said, "It's all right, Frankie. You can come out now."

He waited, but heard nothing from inside the outhouse.

"Frankie? I said you can come out now. D'you hear me, Frankie?"

Longarm glanced around again to make sure Jimmy Jay was not near, then pulled the outhouse door open.

Frankie Powell was still sitting on the crapper with his britches around his ankles.

Longarm did not know if poor Frankie'd had time enough to finish his dump, but if he hadn't done it then he never would. There was a gash in the side of Frankie's neck, and from there down he was painted scarlet with his own blood.

Jimmy Jay's bullet must have passed through the outhouse wall and ripped Frankie's throat out in a macabre accident.

Poor damn Frankie. He had been one unlucky damn gambler. Perhaps it was no wonder he'd had to turn to crime in order to survive. The poor son of a bitch.

Longarm sighed. He would have to go find somebody to tend to the body and the burial. And then he would have to go upstairs and break the news to Cherie.

It was a shame about Frankie. But telling Cherie was going to be a real sonofabitch of a chore. Had to be done, though. Damn it.

Chapter 30

Longarm did not know what was considered proper here, but Frankie did not have any money to pay for his burial. The government would have to do it, and Custis Long would have to front the twenty dollars, since ordinary citizen Henry Smith had no business handing out government payment vouchers. He only hoped the reimbursement would be approved once this job was over and done with.

The undertaker was a man named Smith—George Smith in this case—and Longarm would almost have sworn he had once seen the fellow's rather pudgy likeness on a Wanted poster. That would have been very early though, if at all, back when Longarm was just getting into the business, and he could not be sure of it. He could go through the old flyers when he got back to Denver. There was a box crammed full of them that Henry kept down in the basement.

Or, then again, it could be that he was simply suspicious of anyone who called himself Smith, never mind that an awful lot of folks really did carry that name. This particular Smith doubled as Hyde Junction's undertaker and its dentist.

"I will see to the embalming this very afternoon, cousin," undertaker Smith said to charlatan Smith. "I can assure you that I employ the most thoroughly modern methods and use only the freshest and most effective chemicals in the preservation process.

"Your fee includes preparation of the, um, dearly departed. Washing, shave, all the usual sort of thing. It also includes a sheet to drape the, um, remains for viewing. His clothing seems rather the worse for wear, if you see what I mean. I doubt the blood would wash out easily, and that cloth." Smith shook his head. "Not the best quality, I am sorry to say. But the sheet will suffice. You will want to have a viewing, I presume?"

It was not something Longarm had really thought about. "Yes. Of course we'll have a viewing." If nothing else that would allow Cherie an opportunity to say her good-byes. And, hell, there might be other ne'er-do-wells over there at the hotel who would want to say good-bye to Frankie.

"Do you have a place in mind for the viewing, or would you care to make use of our visitation parlor? There is no additional charge for that."

"Your parlor will be just fine, I'm sure," Longarm said.

"If you want a permanent marker that will be three dollars extra," Smith was saying. "I have several very handsome models to choose from, both granite and marble."

"What comes with the, uh, regular?"

"That would be wood, sir. I do use tight-grained oak heartwood, however. It lasts very nicely. And I carve the deceased's name and dates into the marker. You say the gentleman's name is Powell?"

"Frankie Powell, that's right."

"Frank? Francis? Franklin?"

"I'll have to get back with you about that. All I ever knew him by was Frankie."

"Very well. And his date of birth?"

Longarm could only shrug.

"I see. Well, in a pinch we can make do with a simple date of death. We do know that, don't we, ha ha."

Longarm was not laughing.

"Yes, well, um . . ." Smith glanced at a clock that was ticking laboriously away on the wall. "It is too late for me to open the parlor for his viewing today. Would tomorrow morning do?"

"That would be fine."

"Burial to be concluded on the third day? That would be customary."

"That'd be just fine, then."

"Now, there is the question of, um, payment. I think you will find it understandable that I require payment in advance of the services being performed."

Longarm dug into his britches and came out with a pair of ten-dollar eagles that he handed to Smith. The man beamed with pleasure. But then, this was a small town. Likely he did not get all that much trade here. In either of his lines of endeavor.

"I shall prepare the gentleman this afternoon and evening," Smith said, "and open the doors for viewing at nine o'clock tomorrow morning then, Cousin Smith."

"That's fine." Longarm shook the man's hand—maybe it was only his imagination, but Smith's hand sure did feel cold and clammy to him; kinda like that of a corpse—and headed back toward the hotel.

Very carefully back toward the hotel. That son of a bitch Jimmy Jay had found himself another rifle, damn him, and he was out there someplace.

Chapter 31

Longarm expected hysterics from Cherie. It turned out the girl was much more realistic than that. Cherie's comment when he told her was a simple, heartfelt, "Well, shit!"

If anything Ruby seemed more shocked by the unexpected death than Cherie did. Ruby looked as if she might cry. Cherie just looked like she had forgotten how to cry.

"I don't suppose he had anything in his pockets," Cherie said.

"Like what?"

"Like money, of course."

"He was broke, Cherie. You know that."

"I figured he might've been holding something out on me. No money, huh?"

"Not a cent," Longarm told her. "Not even a watch."

"He used to have a watch but he hocked it. Only got fifty cents for it, and I think the guy at the pawn shop was being generous at that. Frankie said the watch was valuable, but you know what a damn liar he was."

"Was Powell his real name?"

"As far as I know it was."

"What about his proper first name?"

Cherie shrugged. "Frankie. That's all I knew him by. Frankie Powell. No middle name."

"Date of birth?" Longarm asked.

"Damn if I know. He used to tell a bunch of different ages, depending on who he was talking to and what he wanted them to think."

"All right. I'll tell the undertaker and he can do whatever he thinks is right."

"Did you tell Ben?" Cherie asked.

"No, I wanted you to know before anyone else."

"Ben was about as close to Frankie as anybody. You say there's gonna be a viewing?"

Longarm nodded.

"I'll ask Ben to post a notice or something so's our friends can go by and give him a send-off."

"That would be nice." It would also, Longarm thought, be mighty convenient. Among the faces that he would recognize there might well be somebody whose tail he could twist hard enough to make them give up Jimmy Jay. Not that he had the authority to bargain with a felon for the son of a bitch's release. But a little creative thinking never hurt.

Never hurt if Billy Vail did not find out about it, anyway.

Longarm pulled out a cheroot and lit it.

"Do you wanna walk me downstairs so's I can talk to Ben now?" Cherie asked.

"Ruby will take you," Longarm said. "I want to sit at the window here and smoke a little. Maybe look to see if I can spot Jimmy Jay out there someplace."

Cherie frowned a little. So did Ruby.

"Dammit," Longarm snapped at them, "I could use a little help here without the two of you getting the vapors or something. Go on now, please. And Ruby, don't think Cherie is any less likely to sneak away on her own now that Frankie is gone. If anything I'd say she has even less reason to stay now than she did before."

"Yes, sir."

Longarm was not immediately certain he'd heard that correctly. *Sir*? Ruby Bradbury called him "sir"? *Shee-it!*

If he wanted any proof that things were not going along their normal path, that right there would do it.

Sir!

Be damn.

Longarm ignored the two women and pulled a chair over beside the hotel room window, where he could have a good field of view.

But not, unfortunately, much of a field of fire since his rifle was back in Denver, leaving him with only his Colt and the little derringer, while Jimmy Jay once again was armed with a rifle.

Chapter 32

Longarm tapped lightly on the door that connected the two hotel rooms. "Are you ready?"

"Just a minute," an indistinct voice responded. It could have been either woman answering. Not that it made any difference. The two of them had had forty-five minutes to get ready to go down to supper. And they still were not ready.

Longarm shook his head. They were only going down to the hotel dining room, for crying out loud, not getting ready for the grand cotillion or some damn thing. Women!

At least both of them seemed to have gotten over Frankie's death. He hadn't expected Ruby to be much bothered. After all, she had not liked the man very much to begin with. But Cherie's casual acceptance of her paramour's loss surprised him. He had thought Cherie's sun rose and set on Frankie Powell's whims.

He knocked on the door again, louder this time. The two girls might be having a fine time in there fussing with each other's hair or something, but he was getting hungry. "Aren't you ready yet?"

"Coming," a syrupy-sweet voice called.

A moment later the door opened and the room was

filled with the sharp, vaguely floral smell of perfume. Both women had a faint blush of rouge on their cheeks, and their lips were unnaturally red.

Both, he had to admit, looked almighty good, each in her own way. Cherie was petite and perky. A small stick of feminine dynamite. He could not help remembering the unpleasantly curtailed incident back in Denver, when he'd been about to have the girl, only to be so rudely interrupted by that damn Powell. Cherie had one hell of a fine figure, never mind her short stature.

And Ruby was tarted up to look just as loud and sexy as Cherie. Probably the makeup was Cherie's doing. And the upswept red hair. And that tight bodice that showed off a figure fine enough to make a grown man weep. The woman had a waist as tiny as a wasp's middle with a soft swell of shapely hips below and a bosom that promised much more than a mouthful.

Green, Longarm decided. Ruby's eyes were definitely green. And large. And moist. And her lips were full and looked mighty soft.

Longarm blinked and tried to pay attention to business here.

It did not matter what Cherie Johnson looked like. Did not matter how sexy Ruby Bradbury seemed this evening. Dammit, he was here to work. To find Leo Batson. To put J. Jimmy Jay either in chains or into a coffin. And, while he was at it, to stay alive himself.

He was not here to be looking at his, um, partners and getting a hard-on. Which, duty or no, he had at the moment.

The front of his trousers stood proud, attesting to the effect the two women were having on him.

That wouldn't have been so bad, perhaps, but Ruby happened to notice.

He could see it in her eyes the moment she did for she

got a twinkle in them and her dimples showed as she tried to conceal her amusement.

At least, he thought, she found it funny rather than being shocked or insulted. Maybe she wasn't quite the prude he'd thought she was.

Then Cherie, perhaps following the direction of Ruby's gaze, looked down, too.

Cherie was not as restrained as Ruby, though. She giggled. Then reached down and petted Longarm's rigid pecker through the cloth, stroking it the way one might pet a favorite puppy's head.

"Jeez!" Longarm yelped and spun away.

He heard laughter behind him. It was, fortunately, enough of a distraction to eliminate the problem. When he turned back around to face Ruby and Cherie again, his erection had subsided and the front of his britches hung normally.

"Are you sure you're ready to go downstairs now, Mr. Smith?" Cherie asked in a mock serious tone, the laughter lying barely submerged in her voice.

Longarm cleared his throat. "I, um . . . yes, thank you. I think we can go down to supper now."

Chapter 33

Longarm was impressed. Hotel owner Ben Sanders had posted a large signboard in the lobby, notifying his guests about the unexpected death of "friend to all" Frankie Powell. It was a nice gesture on Sanders's part, Longarm thought. Hell, maybe the little weasel had more friends than Longarm ever suspected.

"Mr. Smith," Sanders hailed, as Longarm and the two women came down the stairs. "Mr. Smith?"

"Psst. That's you, y'know," Cherie whispered, nudging him with her elbow.

"Oh. Right." Longarm left the girls waiting beside the door into the dining room and crossed the lobby to the hotel desk. "Yes, Mr. Sanders?"

"I have a note for you. Here you are, sir."

"Ah. Must be something from the undertaker. Thanks." Longarm stuck the folded piece of paper into his pocket and rejoined the women. He escorted them into the dining room, and the trio followed a waiter to a table in the center of the open room.

"I think over there would be better," Longarm said, pointing to an empty table beside the wall, where he could protect his back while keeping an eye on the comings and goings in the room.

"Yes, of course, sir," the waiter said without batting an eye. But then many of the people who frequented the Hyde Inn would be the sort who would not like the thought of strangers behind them.

Longarm settled both women into chairs with their backs to the room—something that Cherie did not very much like—so he could keep his own back to the wall.

"Before I forget again, Cherie, the fellow who's handling the burying wants to know what Frankie's first name was."

She gave him an odd look. "What a silly question. His name is Frankie."

"No, I mean his real name."

Cherie frowned. "How the fuck should I know. Frankie is the only name I ever heard him go by."

"You don't know if . . . never mind. We'll work it out." Longarm dug into his pocket for the note he'd just received and pulled it out, expecting it to be a reminder from George Smith that he needed that name before he could carve the gravesite marker.

Instead Longarm damn near spit when he unfolded the page and read what was on it.

"Powell was an accident. You will not be. I will find you. Soon."

It was signed with the initial J.

Damn him. Damn that son of a bitch anyway.

The note ruined Longarm's appetite. Not out of fear but from frustration.

One shot, that was all he asked. One good chance to throw a shot at Jimmy Jay. Then they would see who wound up still on his feet. Except Jay was a long-distance assassin, while Longarm's style was belly to belly.

Damn him anyway.

Chapter 34

"Psst! Sir. Do you know Miss Nellie?"

Longarm looked at the youngster who was standing cap in hand with a look of awe on his freckled cheeks. He acted like he had never in his life before now set foot into a hotel dining room. But then, very likely he had not.

"Nellie?" Longarm asked.

"There's some calls her 'Buttonhook,' Sir. Do you know her?"

"Oh. Yes. I do."

"Miss Nellie said I should look for somebody that looks like you and ask. She said she can't remember your name."

Good girl, Longarm thought. She could not remember that he was calling himself Henry Smith here—hell, he couldn't remember that himself half the time—but she knew better than to go looking for him under his own name.

Longarm nodded and started reaching into his pocket for a coin to give to the boy. "I'm the one you're looking for. Is there a message for me, son?"

"Yes, sir. She said she wants to see you about the thing you asked her about. If that makes any sense."

Longarm jumped to his feet, abandoning the meal that had only then been delivered to their table. "Here, boy. Sit down. Have something to eat." He was doing more than merely treating the kid to what to him would be a luxury. He did not want the boy walking beside him. He wanted no accidental deaths like what had happened to Frankie Powell.

He dragged a ten-dollar gold piece from his pocket and gave it to Ruby. "I have to go. You can pay for everything, then take Cherie upstairs and wait for me in your room."

"Is there anything I can do?"

"Yes, dammit. I just told you what it is. Now enjoy your meal. All three of you."

Ruby looked resigned but amenable. Cherie looked impatient; obviously she had had something else in mind for the evening. And the messenger boy looked like he'd just stepped into the most exciting moment of his young life, dining in a real hotel restaurant . . . and in the company of two exotic grownup women, too. This was an event he probably would be talking about for years to come.

Longarm handed the boy a nickel and without conscious thought brushed the tips of his fingers over the butt of his Colt to reassure himself that all was in place. Just in case. He dropped his napkin into the kid's lap and headed for the door in long strides.

It was almost full dark when he stepped outside. The lamps in the Hyde Inn lobby were already lit. They would silhouette him perfectly, and he could not help but wonder if Jimmy Jay lay somewhere not too far off, with his eye lining up the sights of a rifle.

Longarm moved quickly to the side to get out of the light. Somewhere in the town he could hear the voices of children noisily finishing up whatever games they had been playing before they returned to their homes for supper. A dog barked. A door slammed.

No one shot at him.

Longarm scowled, angry with himself for allowing that son of a bitch to bother him like this.

Then he hurried away down the street toward Buttonhook Nellie's house of ill—but damned fun—repute.

"You came right away," Nellie said.

"This is important to me, if you have the information I asked for."

"I might. Go into my office. I'll be there in a minute."

With anyone else Longarm might have been suspicious of a trap, that being the reason Nellie did not accompany him. He had known Nellie for a long time, though. He trusted her.

Mostly. Trust or no, he was cautious when he opened her office door.

No one was lurking inside. No gun shots came flying at him out of the room.

Nellie was as good as her word. She did join him in a few moments. She had one of her girls with her, a plump blonde girl with broad features and tiny tits. She had her hair up in pigtails and wore a little white apron over an ordinary housedress. The girl looked like a Scandinavian milkmaid. Which was probably the idea. Longarm guessed she was twenty five but trying to be fifteen again.

On the other hand, she could as easily be fifteen and already aged by her profession so that she looked twenty-five.

"What did you say your name was again, dearie?" Nellie asked.

Longarm reminded her.

"Oh, yes. Now I remember. Mr. Smith, this is Gretchen. Gretchen, Mr. Smith."

The milkmaid curtsied. She had dimples and china-blue eyes. Thick ankles, too, though. Longarm had never

141

been an admirer of thick ankles. Nellie motioned Longarm to a chair and the three of them sat down.

"This afternoon we were asked to open the house earlier than normal," Nellie began. "A gentleman came to the door. He was quite insistent that we allow him to spend time with our dear Gretchen. He offered to pay extra if we allowed him to come inside before our normal working hours."

Longarm pulled out a cheroot and lit it. There was no sense in trying to rush things. Nellie and her girl would get around to telling him about the gentleman caller in their own way and their own time.

"Gretchen agreed to entertain him. He was here for quite some time. It was not until later, until just a little while ago in fact, that I realized he might have been the gentleman you asked me to watch for."

"Oh?" Longarm's interest quickened.

"He was dressed differently, of course. And his hair was closely cropped, not exactly the way you described. But with a change of clothing and before a fresh haircut, Mr. Smith, this man may well have been the party you wanted to see."

Longarm laid his cigar aside and forgot about it. "Gretchen," he said, "I want you to tell me everything you can about this, um, gentleman caller you, uh, entertained this afternoon."

The girl looked at Nellie, who nodded. "Tell him everything, dear. Mr. Smith is a friend. I don't want you to hold a single thing back."

"Yes, ma'am." The girl looked at Longarm and smiled. That was a mistake. She was missing two teeth on the upper left of her mouth, and the effect was not at all attractive. At least not to him. Who knew what someone else might make of it. She turned her attention to Longarm. "You're gonna pay me for my time, Mr. Smith?"

"Gretchen!"

Longarm had never heard Nellie use a tone of voice like that. But obviously Gretchen had. The whore jumped like she'd just been poked with a very sharp stick. Hell, no wonder. Nellie sounded like a cavalry top-sergeant. Longarm would've jumped, too, if Nellie'd spoken to him like that.

It was no wonder, he realized, that sweet Nellie could take command of a house full of dim-witted farm girls and whip them into shape. Nellie had business abilities that he'd never suspected.

"Yes'm, I'm sorry. Sir, you want me to tell you *every-thing*?"

"Indeed I do, Gretchen. Everything."

Chapter 35

"Has this man ever been a, um, a customer here before?"

"I don't remember him," the girl said.

"I can tell you for sure," Nellie put in. "This was his first visit to my house."

"You saw him, too?" Longarm asked.

Nellie shook her head. "I was in the kitchen having breakfast when he arrived. Albert let him in."

Longarm remembered Albert. He supposed Albert would be considered Nellie's servant, although in truth he was much more than that. Albert was a tall, dignified mulatto who was probably getting on in years now. He had been with Nellie forever. Longarm suspected Albert was Nellie's lover as much as her employee. He took charge of the details of running the house, shopping for groceries, arranging for laundry to be done, distributing fresh towels to the rooms—that sort of thing.

"Gretchen," Longarm said, "please tell me what happened."

"He . . ." She looked at Nellie. "Are you sure I have t' do this, ma'am?"

Nellie nodded. "Everything."

"Yes'm." The girl sighed. "You got to understand that

I'm the one that takes the rough customers, mister. I got these tiny tits but I got no feeling in them. Maybe from the way I was beat on so much when I was back home. Anyway, a guy can grab hold and squeeze or slap pretty much all he wants and I won't hardly feel nothing in them. An' I don't mind if a guy squirts in my mouth or wants to fuck me in the ass, see, so whenever there's somebody wanting something, uh, kinda special, they always give him to me 'cause they know I don't give a shit. You know what I'm telling you?"

"Yes, I think I do," Longarm said. "And this man wanted you in particular? Or anyway, wanted the sort of things you could do. He was rough with you?"

"Yeah. Kinda. He wanted to take hold of my titties like he was gonna rip them off me and then he beat on me a little . . . not so awful bad, I've had a lot worse . . . and then he had me get down on my knees an' beg to let me suck his dick. Which I did. Lordy, did that man ever have a load he wanted shut off. I thought he wasn't never gonna quit flowing. I thought I'd gag or puke or something, but o' course I acted like it was the most wonderful thing ever, and that made him happy. When he was done he got dressed without another word and—" she looked rather nervously in Nellie's direction again, "—an' he gave me a tip. Then he left."

"Did he do any talking while he was here?" Longarm asked.

"Yes, sir. A little. He said this was a special day. He didn't say exactly what was special about it. But he was, like, celebrating something."

"Did he have a gun?"

"Sure."

"A little gun or a big one?"

"I never saw it. It was in his coat pocket. I heard the clunk against the chair leg when he hung his coat over the back of the chair in my room. I knew what it was he was carrying. Lots of men do."

"He didn't give you any hints about what was so special today?"

"No, sir."

"Did he have a rifle with him?"

"Oh, no. Just the pistol in his pocket."

Longarm grunted. Something special. That could mean Jimmy Jay intended to meet his new client this evening. Or it could as easily mean he expected to kill Longarm tonight.

"Describe him for me again please."

The girl did, and Longarm had to agree that the gent could well be Jimmy Jay, except with a fresh haircut and a change of clothes. Dammit!

"Long . . . uh, Mr. Smith."

"Yes, Nellie?"

"You might like to know where this man is staying."

Longarm's interest immediately quickened. "You know good and well that I'd want t' know that."

"When he left here, Albert had the presence of mind to follow him. I've written down the information about where you can find him. Or at least where he was late this afternoon. Take this and make good use of it." She handed Longarm a folded slip of paper that he dropped into his pocket.

Longarm beamed. "Nellie, I love you."

"Oh, how I wish you meant that, dear."

"But I do. Just not in quite . . . that way."

"I know. I know." She sighed. "Is there anything more you need from Gretchen, or can I send her back to work now?"

"With directions to where Jay is staying I have everything I need, Nellie." He stood and dragged a dollar-sized Mexican peso from his pocket and gave it to Gretchen. "Thank you for your help."

147

"Yes, sir. Whatever Miss Nellie wants. You know?"

"Sure."

"You can go back to the parlor now, dearie," Nellie said.

Longarm slipped out when Gretchen did. He did not want Nellie to trap him into another roll in the hay. Once a year with roly-poly Buttonhook Nellie was quite enough for any man.

Chapter 36

The directions Albert gave were clear enough. The gent had gone to a room, or perhaps a small flat, on the second floor over a seamstress's shop at the far end of town from the Hyde Inn. It would be an ideal lair for a murderer like Jimmy Jay, Longarm immediately saw.

The only access to the place was a set of stairs on the side of the building. The stair treads were warped and cracking, and no doubt would be noisy. The door at the top of those stairs had a glass panel, so anyone inside not only would be warned of the approach of strangers, they would be able to easily see who was coming. That was an advantage Longarm had no intention of giving to the assassin.

A dim light showed yellow in that glass rectangle now, but that did not tell him if Jay was in there or not. The bastard could have left the light burning low while he went somewhere to eat. Or to lay another ambush.

Longarm stood on the sidewalk across the street from the apartment, chewing the end of an unlighted cheroot while he mulled over his options.

There were not all that many. He could turn and walk away—which he damn well was not going to do—or he could get inside the flat and either kill Jay, if the man was there, or wait for him to return and kill him then. Either way, Longarm wanted Jimmy Jay dead. Or in handcuffs, if he really had to arrest the son of a bitch.

The big question then was whether Jimmy Jay was indeed inside right now. If he was absent, Longarm could simply walk up the stairs without worrying about the amount of noise he made, slip inside, and settle down to wait for Jay's return. But if he were in there ...

Longarm tucked the soggy end of his cigar into the corner of his mouth and unconsciously felt the Colt to make sure it was riding loose and free in the leather. Then he left the street corner where he was loitering and crossed over to the mouth of the alley where the apartment staircase was.

Instead of risking the stairs, though, he continued on to the back of the dressmaker's shop. He grunted with satisfaction when he reached the tiny, trash-strewn yard behind the building.

There was the usual outhouse and a tumbledown shed where no livestock were kept, but which was used now to store a few rusty garden implements, which Longarm determined with the flick of a match flame that he quickly extinguished once he saw Jay was not keeping a horse here.

The good news was that there was a small porch attached to the back of the shop, and above it a window that almost certainly led to the back of Jimmy Jay's flat. That window, unlike the one at the head of the staircase, was dark, suggesting a good possibility that Jay was absent and had left the front room light burning for his return.

Good news indeed, Longarm thought. Now if he could only ...

He went back into the shed and lit another match, this time using it for a more thorough search of the shed's contents. What he really wanted was a ladder. What he got was the same uninteresting collection of rake, spade, hoe, and the like that he'd noticed before. No ladder. Shit!

He blew the match flame out before it burned down to his fingers and stood still for a few moments while his eyes readjusted to the dark, then returned to the yard behind the seamstress's shop.

The only thing he could see that might do him some good was the rain barrel set beside the porch. Now if he could just . . .

He went into the yard next door and found a washtub on the back porch of that building, whatever it was. Borrowing the galvanized steel tub, he returned to the dressmaker's and upended the washtub. The upside-down tub fit rather nicely over top of the rain barrel.

Longarm took hold of the vertical roof support post at the back corner of the porch and stepped up onto the edge of the porch, then onto the now covered rain barrel. He made a little noise doing it, but not enough to worry about. So far, so good.

He shifted the cheroot to the other side of his mouth and took hold of the edge of the porch roof. With a low grunt of effort he pulled himself up, hooked a leg over the edge, and levered himself up until he could roll onto the dry shingles.

The soft crunch of breaking wood told him some of the shingles were breaking. He would be in trouble if the damn things made too much noise or if, heaven forbid, they gave way completely, and he fell through to the porch floor below.

Worried lest he concentrate too much of his weight onto any one spot, he rolled across the roof to the wall of the building before he rose onto his knees and found the apartment window several feet to his right.

Moving cautiously, he crabbed silently in that direction and took his hat off before he peered into the window.

151

A six-inch gap was left open to admit air. Longarm paused there outside the window to listen. He heard nothing from inside the darkened room. A very thin, very faint line of lamplight lay at floor level toward the front of the building, the light in the front room showing beneath a closed door—which suggested this room at the back was a bedroom while the one where the light was would be a parlor or sitting room.

So far, so good.

Longarm very carefully pushed the window up until it was fully open. He managed to do it in silence.

He took the Colt into his hand, then rose to his feet and threw a leg over the window sill, ducking down to let his upper body follow.

A floorboard creaked when he stepped inside, but he still heard nothing inside the apartment.

It was dark inside the room. He could make out no shapes or images, other than the dim fan of light underneath the door in front of him and the pale outline of the window behind.

Gun in hand, Longarm edged on tiptoe across the floor to the doorway, and felt for the doorknob.

There was no quiet or easy way to do this. And if Jimmy Jay was not in the front room, it would not matter what he did anyway, so he might just as well assume the worst and try to disorient the SOB.

Longarm braced himself, then jerked the bedroom door open and let out an earsplitting howl as he leaped through with the Colt leveled in search of a target.

Chapter 37

"Jesus God!" the man seated in the armchair cried out in alarm and dropped the Bible he'd been reading.

"Oh, damn," Longarm responded. "I . . . there's been a mistake. I'm sorry. I . . ."

He heard a faint thump behind him.

Then heard a mighty thump. Inside his head.

Something very solid and very heavy smashed down onto the back of his head, and Longarm felt himself begin to fall.

He was no longer conscious when he ended that fall on the floor of the apartment he'd just broken into.

Longarm woke to find himself lying on his side on the bare wooden floor, trussed hand and foot. The man and a large—a *very* large—woman were standing over him. The man was rather awkwardly holding a revolver that looked suspiciously like Longarm's own. He looked like he would not know how to operate the Colt if he had to. The woman, however, had a firm and competent grip on the handle of a cast-iron skillet. She looked like she knew exactly what to do with that if she need to. Longarm gathered it was the skillet that had laid him low.

"Who are you?" "Who are you?" Longarm and the man spoke simultaneously, their voices blending together as if one.

"You go first," Longarm offered.

"Don't you bother to find out who your victims are?" the man countered.

"I thought you were someone else," Longarm told him. "Sorry if I frightened you."

"It will be a cold day you-know-where before I am frightened by the likes of you," the woman declared. "I have the protection of a host of angels. You and your kind cannot intimidate me."

Longarm believed her. She looked pissed off maybe, but not the least bit frightened. "You hit me with that thing?"

"I did. And I shall do so again if you offer any trouble before the marshal arrives."

"You called the marshal?"

"We sent for him."

"Luella," the man said in a cautionary tone.

"All right. But we intend to send for him. We just thought . . . we thought we might have killed you. Sam wanted to see about that before either of us left to bring the marshal."

Longarm's head felt like it was splitting in two. He did not feel any sticky, wet ooze inside his shirt though, and did not smell any blood. He guessed that the stupid-looking hat had protected him from worse injury. "You might well have killed me with that thing," he said, gesturing with his chin at the skillet in Luella's ham-sized fist. Lordy, but that was one big woman. Not fat. Just big. The man was of normal proportions. He did not look very much like J. Jimmy Jay though. Same height and hair color. Apparently that was enough to arouse Gretchen's suspicions. He could see how she'd made the mistake. He supposed. Dammit.

154

"Can I sit up? I feel like I been bruised over half my body."

"You did fall rather hard," Sam said.

The two of them took him by the shoulders and dragged him into a sitting position.

"That's better, thanks. Now who the hell are you?"

"Please do not use foul language in our presence," Luella growled.

"Yes, ma'am." He gave the skillet a wary eye, worried that she might decide to whack him with it again.

"I am the Reverend Samuel Alexander Persons," Samuel Alexander Persons said. "This is my wife, Sister Luella Pembrook Persons. You may be familiar with our work?" Sam sounded mildly hopeful when he said that. "We are engaged in a movement of evangelistic revival. We have only recently arrived in Hyde's Junction and shall begin our labors here this coming Sabbath. Surely you are familiar with our labors."

"Sorry. But then, I travel a lot. Don't have much time for churchgoing."

Luella sniffed. "I should think you do not. The sort of man who invades the homes of innocents. Undoubtedly would have robbed us. God knows what vile uses you would have made of me." Longarm thought he detected a note of mild hope in her voice, too, when she said that.

The truth was that he could not imagine any sober male human wanting to take Sister Luella to bed with carnal intent. The woman had a mustache, he saw now that he was able to get his thoughts together and pay attention. And she was . . . well, the truth was that the poor thing was as homely as a hog wallow.

Ruby Bradbury was big, but she was pretty. And sexy. Luella was big but she was . . . just big.

Sam was about half Sister Luella's size and seemed rather timid. Longarm had a momentary image in his mind of the Rev. Samuel whateverthefuck Persons rutting on top of Buttonhook Nellie's girl, Gretchen. It was almost enough to start him laughing out loud.

Not that Longarm could blame the poor bastard for preferring Gretchen. Not hardly.

"Could I give you folks a piece of advice?" Longarm asked.

The two looked puzzled.

"Next time you hog-tie somebody, learn t' do it right." He reached up and retrieved his Colt from Sam, shoved it back into its holster, and then set about stripping the wraps of thin cord off his ankles.

Luella stepped back and raised her skillet as if to strike again. Sam just looked confused, as if he really did not understand how the gun had gotten out of his hand and into Longarm's.

"It's all right," Longarm said as he came to his feet and stretched his aching limbs. "I'm a deputy marshal. But I want you to keep quiet about that. I'm here working undercover, and I can't let anybody know who I really am. D'you understand that?"

"No," Sam confessed.

"Sister, would you please put your weapon away now an' accept my apologies for interruptin' your evening. Sam, I'd like to have a few words with you. In private if you don't mind. I don't want to, um, offend the sensibilities of the good lady here."

What he did not want to do, of course, was to tell Luella that ol' Sam was getting a little afternoon stress relief in a whorehouse.

"How do we know you are a deputy marshal?" Luella asked suspiciously.

Longarm sighed and pulled out his badge.

"Custis Long?"

"That's right, but I'm using a different name here. Please. Both of you forget about me, would you, please?

Don't say anything to anybody about ever meeting me. I think that would be for the best."

"Well, I don't know," Luella said. "We are very honest people, you know."

"Yes, Sister, but I'm reasonably sure nobody's gonna walk up to you and ask did some deputy break into your place last night an' did you try and kill him when he did. I'm not asking you t' lie, see. Just don't bring it up. Nobody else is going to, so don't you say nothing either."

"I just don't know what to say," Luella said.

"Sam will explain everything to you later, I'm sure. Sam. Come with me, please. Downstairs."

Sam looked puzzled, but he retrieved his shoes and his coat, then followed Longarm down to the street.

Longarm explained things. In a very low voice that would not carry up to Luella's ears.

"Oh, I . . . I . . . oh, dear," Sam said, thoroughly flustered by the idea that his afternoon pursuits were known. "Oh, please . . ."

"Sam, I got no intention of saying anything to anybody about you. I'm asking you in return t' not say anything to anybody about me. Does that sound fair to you?"

"Yes. Please. Anything. Just don't . . ."

"Not a word," Longarm assured him. "Not a word."

He meant that, too. Deputy United States Marshal Custis Long had absolutely no desire to go telling anyone about the time a woman with a frying pan had gotten the best of him.

Longarm extended his hand to shake on the agreement. Silence was, after all, golden.

"And extended my apologies, once again, t' your good, um, wife," he said. "I'm sure you can see how I'd've made the mistake."

"Yes, but . . . those people. Over there. You know who I mean. They won't . . ."

"Not a word, Sam. They won't tell on you, neither. In

fact, if it makes you feel any better, I won't tell even them who you really are. Just that you aren't the hired killer I thought you was. Why, knowing they've made such a mistake an' put you in danger, they might just treat you real special the next time you drop by to, uh, minister to them. I'll even suggest that to Nellie."

Sam brightened considerably at that thought. He was smiling quite happily when he told Longarm good night and returned upstairs to the waiting arms of Sister Luella whateverthefuck Persons.

Wonderful couple, Longarm thought on his way back to the hotel. Salt of the earth. You bet.

Chapter 38

When he got back to the hotel—without being shot at or otherwise molested—Longarm stopped in for a drink before going upstairs. He saw two more men he was pretty sure were on Wanted posters, but neither one of them was a big enough fish to justify him violating his orders so he could arrest them. He really was going to have to bring a bunch of boys back here though and throw a net over this whole shebang. A raid on any given Saturday night should result in a very nice haul of criminals, he suspected.

With that happy thought in mind he waved a cheerful goodnight to his hotel-keeping host, Mr. Benjamin Sanders, and went up to a room that still contained lingering scents of Frankie Powell in it.

He tapped on the connecting door and got a mumbled response to assure him that Cherie and Ruby were there and all was well. Then Longarm got undressed, sat by the window in the dark room while he smoked a final cheroot, and went quietly to bed.

He had not yet had time enough to drop off to sleep when he heard the faint creak of door hinges being opened.

Longarm lifted the Colt out of its holster, which was

hanging on the bedpost, and waited. If Jimmy Jay was coming in . . .

It was not Jimmy Jay, but someone did indeed enter. A pale form crept stealthily in from the women's room. A very pale very small figure, meaning it had to be Cherie.

As she approached Longarm's bed there was enough moonlight seeping in through the open window to show that she was naked. And every bit as nicely put together as he remembered from that day back in Denver when she made the mistake of picking him for a mark.

Damn, but she'd had him worked up that afternoon.

Seeing her now brought the feeling back. She was petite. She was pretty. She was *not*, he suspected, as horny as she was likely to pretend.

What was happening here, Longarm guessed, was that Cherie was looking for a place of refuge, so to speak. Her protector and provider had been Frankie. Now Frankie was dead, and Cherie wanted someone to take Powell's place. She wanted someone to take care of her, and Deputy U.S. Marshal Custis Long looked like a good candidate for the job.

She would be wanting security, he knew. Not love. For a woman alone with no family to fall back on, security was far more important than love.

Toward that end, of course, Cherie would have to give Longarm a reason to keep her around. And the tools of Cherie's trade consisted of two tits, one pussy, and one warm and willing mouth. The girl, he was pretty sure, intended to use what she had to give him such a good night that he would be hankering for more.

It wouldn't work.

But Cherie Johnson was a grown-up girl. She was no virgin. Not hardly. And anyway, who was he to deny her a chance to make her play?

Longarm pushed the Colt back into its leather. That

was not the sort of gun and that holster not the kind of sheath that would be needed here tonight.

"Don't tell me you got lost looking for the thunder mug in the dark," he said with a grin, as he dragged the sheet back and moved over to make room for her on the bed.

Chapter 39

"Lie back. Let me," Cherie ordered.

And who was he to argue with a lady? Longarm lay back and let her take charge.

"Close your eyes."

He did, and a moment later felt the faint warmth of her breath on his skin. Then the touch of her tongue, wet and faintly rasping, like a softer and more gentle cat's tongue.

She started at his belly. Worked up his side—that tickled, dammit—to his armpit. She nuzzled him there and he could hear Cherie breathing in his scent before she licked him there as well. The sensation was unexpectedly arousing.

As if he needed arousing any further. He was already hard as marble and throbbing with every beat of his heart.

Cherie's very busy tongue roved across his throat. Explored inside one ear and then the other. Drifted downward.

When she licked and suckled his right nipple the sensation shot all the way down into his crotch. She stayed there for a considerable time, and he came remarkably close to coming without her ever once touching his cock.

She moved over to the other nipple and gave it full attention, then slowly licked her way down his belly, paused to probe inside his navel with the tip of that delightful tongue, then continued on her way.

"Ah! Oh, geez. Shit. Yes!" When finally she hovered over the tip of his pecker almost but not quite touching him, he could feel the heat of her breath again. It was all he could do to keep from grabbing the back of her head and shoving her down onto his sword.

Cherie bent lower and touched the head of his cock with the tip of her tongue, ran her tongue around and around, then opened her mouth wide and sank gently onto his shaft, taking it past her mouth and into her throat.

She gagged a little, but only a little, and Longarm thought he was going to jump out of his skin. She surrounded him with the moist heat of her mouth, and his hips involuntarily rose to press himself even deeper into her.

"Ah! Lordy." Longarm began to pump his hips but he did not have time to make more than two thrusts before Cherie withdrew and with a knowing feline smile straddled his waist.

She reached down to pull Longarm's wet cock away from the crack of her ass and hold it upright so she could impale herself on it.

This time Cherie was the one who gasped when he filled her. She braced the palms of both hands on his chest and began to work her hips in a slow, circular motion, grinding herself onto him, her head thrown back and a blank, distant look on her face as her thoughts and feelings were drawn deep inside herself in total concentration on the pleasure that she was taking as much as she was giving.

Longarm noticed this, then closed his eyes again and let Cherie grind and moan.

He was already built almost to the bursting point, and

it seemed that Cherie was more than ready to explode, as well. After only a few seconds the rhythm of Cherie's motion quickened and her breathing became rapid and shallow.

Longarm felt the rise of sap deep in his balls and tried to hold still, but could not. In the final moments before his massive climax his hips rose wildly to meet her. He pummeled and battered her with powerful strokes, then came with a shout and a spurt of hot, milky semen that filled Cherie's pussy and ran back out onto Longarm's cock and his balls.

Cherie climaxed at the same time. Her eyes rolled back and she cried aloud, then collapsed onto his chest.

He could feel her breath on his still moist left nipple. Within seconds Cherie began very softly to snore. She was asleep, lying on top of him, his cock still plunged deep inside her body.

She was sated. But then, so was he.

Longarm smiled.

Then felt a sudden alarm as the side of the bed shifted as weight was added to it even though Cherie was on top of him sound asleep.

Chapter 40

"Ruby! What the hell are you . . . ?"

Longarm gaped in sheer disbelief. The big jail matron was as naked as Cherie. And she was gorgeous. He'd known she was pretty and that she was built, but . . .

Big as her tits were they were in perfect proportion to the rest of her body. They stood tall and proud, with dark red nipples like cherries sitting atop cones of pale ice cream,

Her rib cage was sharply defined, sloping inward to a waist that seemed impossibly small and a belly that was almost as flat as a man's.

Her legs were long and sleek, her calves shapely and her ankles small.

Her pussy hair had been trimmed so short it was nearly nonexistent, and he could plainly see the puffy flaps of her pussy lips peeking out of that scanty patch of hair.

She was . . . damn, but she was pretty.

Longarm was still inside Cherie. His cock began to swell and grow again when he looked at Ruby.

Cherie awakened with a smile and reached behind to take Ruby's hand and pull her down onto the bed beside Longarm. "You came," she said.

"Yes."

"You promised," Cherie said.

"I haven't forgotten. I'll try. I really will."

Cherie lifted her hips, allowing Longarm's cock to slide free of her snatch. The air on it felt chilly.

Cherie shifted down toward the foot of the bed so that she was kneeling between Longarm's legs. She smiled and beckoned Ruby closer, and the big girl sighed and moved down so that she lay with her head beside Longarm's waist.

"Remember how I told you and try it now," Cherie urged.

Longarm had no idea what the fuck the two were talking about. But he certainly knew what Ruby was doing. She leaned over and rather tentatively touched the head of his cock with her tongue.

"It tastes a little sweet," she observed.

"That's his own cum," Cherie explained. "He came inside me just a minute ago. He still has his juice on it."

"Oh." Ruby blinked and tilted her head first one way, then the other, as she examined Longarm's prick as if she'd never seen one before, at least not this close up.

"Go on now. Touch his balls. Hold them like I told you."

Ruby cupped Longarm's cods inside the curl of her fingers. Her touch was light and he thought a little awkward.

"Now the cock. Just the head at first."

"Do you think . . . ?"

"Do it, Ruby. Like I told you."

"All right." Ruby's lips parted and she slid them over the head of Longarm's cock.

"Ouch, dammit."

Ruby jumped and pulled instantly away.

"What did I tell you about your teeth?" Cherie cautioned.

"I forgot," Ruby said.

"Go on now. Try it again."

Ruby took the bulbous head of Longarm's prick into her mouth.

"See?" Cherie said.

Ruby raised her head, releasing his pecker. "It isn't bad, actually."

"That's right. It's flesh. Just like sucking on a nipple except a lot bigger, that's all."

"I don't know,"

"Of course you do. You're just being obstinate. Go ahead now. Suck it. Nice and deep this time."

Ruby did, taking about half of Longarm's shaft into her mouth. She made no effort to take it all the way into her throat, and he was rather pleased that she did not. He could feel her begin to gag from taking it as far in as she already had.

"Now the other," Cherie said.

"But, dear. Please!"

"You promised. You have to at least try."

"All right."

Cherie moved aside, leaving her place between Longarm's legs and moving over while Ruby straddled him.

It was Cherie who reached between Longarm's legs to capture his prick and guide it to the lips of Ruby's pussy.

"Squat down now. Lower. Lower."

Longarm could feel the heat of Ruby's body engulf the head of his cock. The big woman was tight. Amazingly tight. She . . . well, shit, he thought, finally figuring it out.

"You've never been with a man before, have you?" he blurted.

"Do you mind?"

"Not if you don't. But I'm surprised. Mighty surprised."

"I promised Cherie I would try it."

"Hush, both of you. Let down, Ruby. All the way. Take him all the way in now."

"It hurts," Ruby pouted.

"Give it a minute. If you can take a hairbrush in there you can damn sure take a man."

"A *hairbrush*?" Longarm yelped.

"Just the handle, silly," Ruby told him as she lowered herself the rest of the way onto Longarm's handle. Damn, but she was tight. No wonder, too, if she was a virgin. Well, sort of a virgin. Apparently he was the first human male to be in there, but this was not the first time she'd had that particular cavity filled.

"Now move. Pump. That's right. Grind. Round and round, Ruby. Up and down. Now you're getting it."

"It doesn't feel bad."

"But does it feel good?"

Ruby shrugged. "It doesn't feel bad. What the hell more do you want?"

"Longarm dear, how are you doing?" Cherie asked.

"Confused."

"Can you come again?"

"Sure, but . . ."

"Keep going, Ruby. Bring him off."

"He's going to shoot that stuff inside my body?"

"Yes, of course."

"It could make me pregnant."

"He used up most of his stuff in me already. You'll be all right."

"No, dammit, I don't want to take a chance on getting pregnant. How could I hold my job if I got pregnant?"

"Then bring him off with your mouth. You can't get knocked up that way."

"And swallow it?"

"You don't have to if you don't want to. Just hold it in your mouth until you can spit it out."

Longarm felt like he was being examined in a damn

doctor's office or something. Like he wasn't really there, just some object that the two women needed for a few minutes of instruction.

"Jesus!" he blurted.

"Be quiet," Cherie chided him. "Ruby, which way do you want? Remember now. You did promise."

"So did you," Ruby said rather sulkily.

"I haven't forgotten."

Ruby sighed again. Then she pulled back, dropping him out of the tight hold of her cunt. She knelt between his legs and took him into her mouth.

"That's right," Cherie encouraged. "Now, do it just like I told you. But remember. Careful with those teeth. And let your tongue do most of the work for you."

Cherie reached in to cup his balls in her hand. He could feel the scrape of one fingernail moving delicately back and forth on his asshole.

Ruby took him into her mouth and began to suck, slurping noisily as she lifted her head and then dipped it down again. Lifted and dipped. Lifted and dipped.

After a few minutes Longarm again felt that familiar and much cherished building of pressure deep inside his groin. Filling his balls. Bursting outward in a rush.

At the last instant he was unable to hold still any longer. He thrust powerfully upward in his spasm of release, driving himself deep into Ruby's throat for the first time and spilling his seed there.

"Ah! I swallowed it. Oh shit, I swallowed it." She slapped Longarm's chest. Hard. "Damn you, I swallowed it."

"It isn't gonna hurt nothing," Cherie said. "It's only a little cum. Why, I bet I've drunk gallons of the stuff. I *like* it."

"Well I don't," Ruby said, pouting again.

"It's over now. You won't have to do it again."

"Promise?"

"Yes," Cherie assured her.

The two women got up, totally ignoring Longarm, who still lay naked and sprawled on his back on the rumpled hotel bed.

Ruby took Cherie's hand and led the petite blonde back into their own room. She pulled the door closed behind her, and a moment later Longarm heard the snick of a deadbolt being shut to lock the connecting door between the two rooms.

He could not actually have sworn in a court of law that he knew what just happened in this room.

But he sure thought he understood it.

And what the hell. It was their lives. Their choices. Seemed a helluva waste, though. Ruby was pretty and could've been mighty good if she'd had the yen for it.

Longarm got up, washed the residues off himself with water from the pitcher and basin, then went to sleep feeling rather completely sated.

Sure was a waste though, Ruby being like she was.

Chapter 41

Cherie cried on their way to the undertaker's parlor, although Longarm doubted it was Frankie Powell the girl was weeping for but likely the downturn her own life had taken. For by morning it was clear that Cherie had her new protector to take Frankie's place.

Ruby touched Cherie and fondled her and fussed over her like a husband with his new bride. Which, Longarm supposed, the two of them were . . . kind of. Ruby was the man of the family; Cherie was the girl, and that was just the way it was.

Longarm was not shocked exactly. He had seen such things before. But he did not approve of it, either.

Still, it was none of his damn business. And in a way it made his job easier. Cherie was not about to try getting away from Ruby now.

Frankie's funeral service was scheduled for 1 P.M., according to the notice posted on a chalkboard in the lobby of the Hyde Inn. Longarm reminded himself that he still had to speak with George Smith about the name to be carved on the marker. They would just have to go with Frankie. Either that or make it "F. Powell." Longarm had no idea which of those would be considered proper in a case like this. Hopefully, Smith would know.

The three of them walked down Main with Longarm on the street side of the sidewalk, Ruby close to the buildings and tiny Cherie sandwiched between them. And thinking about Cherie being between the two others . . . Longarm glanced toward Ruby. He still thought it was a helluva waste, her being the way she was.

"In here, ladies," Longarm said, removing his derby at the entrance to the funeral parlor and holding the door for Ruby and Cherie.

He was amazed at how many people had signed the guest register in the brief time since Frankie had died. Obviously the little gambler had more friends than Longarm would have suspected. A good many of them were crowded into the parlor now, dressed in their Sunday best. Or in the case of most of these, he guessed, their Saturday night best. It was a rough-looking crowd and he suspected every one of them had already served prison time—and likely would again when the law got around to catching them.

Just from the ones Longarm recognized, he saw that a bounty hunter could have retired on the proceeds if he could throw a loop over this roomful and collect all the outstanding rewards on the men and the handful of women here.

There was no preacher as such, but George Smith, wearing a black suit and a dolefully somber expression, delivered a eulogy that was long on generalities and mighty short on specifics about the departed. Longarm gathered this was what passed for a standardized speech in the undertaking business. If you don't know what to say, mouth something nice. Meaningless, of course. But nice.

Cherie was the only one in the room who shed actual tears, although a number of the men seemed to be genuinely saddened by the passing of Frankie Powell.

When the eulogizing was over and done with, Smith announced that the burial would be at the town cemetery, immediately following. There was a scraping of chairs and reaching for hats as everyone stood and began shuffling out.

Longarm and Ruby stood at the door beside Cherie while the mourners passed by to offer condolences, Cherie being as close to family as Frankie had had. If the man had any real family anywhere in the country, no one knew who they might be.

Sad when you considered that, Longarm thought.

He stood there looking almost as solemn as George Smith had, listening with half an ear while the folks spoke softly to Cherie and filed outside.

"Thank you, Leo. Thank you for coming."

That caught Longarm's attention for damn sure.

Leo. As in Leo Batson? Well, shit. It looked like Frankie had led him to the Mail Bomber after all. Not exactly in the way Frankie planned. But even so . . .

Leo was a very ordinary-looking fellow. He wore spectacles and a suit that looked as if it had come off some clothier's shelf instead of being properly fitted and sewn. The man had a bald spot that occupied the back third or so of his head, and his shoulders had that rounded look that suggested a softness of body. To look at him, one would think he might have been a store clerk or an amanuensis.

And this was the man who was disrupting the mails and striking fear into the hearts of politicians across half the country? *Shee-it!*

"Cherie? I don't believe I know this gentleman," Longarm said.

"Henry, this is our dear, dear friend, Leo Batson. Leo, this is Henry Smith. Henry was . . . ," Cherie sobbed and dabbed at her eyes before going on. "Henry was Frankie's last partner."

"Please accept my sympathies, Mr. Smith. So sorry we have to meet under these, um, circumstances."

"Yes," Longarm said sorrowfully. "Could I possibly speak with you after the graveside ceremony?"

Batson looked mildly surprised. "Why . . . yes, I suppose so." He shifted his attention. Longarm could see that Batson's eyes were on Cherie's tits, which stood out quite nicely above a very tightly cinched waist. "You will be there too, dear?"

"Of course, Leo." She went onto tiptoe to deliver a kiss onto Batson's cheek. Longarm didn't mind, but Ruby looked like she wanted to spit.

"In that case, Cherie, you know I'll be there."

"Thank you, Leo. Thank you for coming."

Batson joined the others who were leaving, most turning in the direction of the hotel but a stalwart few going the other way, toward the cemetery.

Longarm felt a sadness. Poor damn Frankie. He rather doubted Frankie would consider his sacrifice worthwhile, even though it appeared that Longarm had his man now, or damned soon would.

Still, this was what they'd come for. Longarm supposed he ought to be pleased.

He wasn't.

Chapter 42

They could bury Frankie without Longarm arresting Leo
Batson and disrupting things, he decided. He owed the
man that much, anyway. A decent burial at the end of the
road was the very least Longarm figured he could do for
Frankie now.

And anyway, Batson was one of the few who were
going to the cemetery.

Everyone walked slowly in that direction, moving as
individuals rather than in a group, the dozen or so of them
strung out along the side of the road in no particular order,
depending on who had been first out the door back at the
undertaking parlor.

Longarm, Ruby, and Cherie had to tag along behind
after standing at the door to accept sympathies until the
last of Frankie's mourners left.

George Smith and a Negro helper passed them in the
hearse before they had gone two hundred yards. They had
been quick to close the coffin and load it into the glass-
sided hearse. Smith's pair of horses pulling the light
hearse, Longarm noticed, were handsome critters, but they
were grays, not the traditional black animals.

Longarm kept his attention on Leo Batson, who was

walking about forty yards ahead. He expected to collar the man as soon as the burying was done with.

He was also trying to keep a wary eye out for Jimmy Jay. The time and place for Frankie's burial were hardly secret. Jay was certain to know. He might very well be lying in wait somewhere nearby, ready to take his shot at Longarm.

The cemetery was on the side of town farthest away from the railroad and not too terribly far from the hotel.

The mourners reached the patch of thin weeds and weathered headstones, and began to gather in a loose group around a newly dug grave. The hearse had already backed up to it by the time Longarm and the women arrived. Several of the men in the group helped Smith and his worker get the coffin out of the hearse and down onto a set of poles laid over the open grave. Later, after everyone else was gone, Smith would lower the coffin into the earth—or simply drop it, more than likely—and cover it over.

For now, though, the pine box lay atop the waiting grave. As soon as Cherie was there, Smith removed the coffin lid and allowed everyone to pass and look at the deceased one last time, with Cherie being the first to do so.

"Ashes to ashes; dust to dust," Smith intoned when everyone had had his chance to see that it was indeed Frankie Powell inside the box. Then Smith and his helper set the lid back in place, and Smith pounded one nail in at each end. They would finish that job, too, after everyone left.

"Miss Johnson, is there anything you would like to say?"

Cherie shook her head. She was crying again, and Ruby was squeezing her hand in an attempt to comfort her.

"Bow your heads, please."

178

Everyone did so. Except Longarm. He continued to rake the surrounding area with his eyes lest Jimmy Jay take this opportunity to . . .

"Shit!" he yelped in the middle of George Smith's prayer.

A puff of dust—or perhaps it was a wisp of gun smoke rising from the muzzle of a rifle—appeared at the side of a tuft of sage a hundred yards or so out onto the empty Nebraska prairie.

Longarm grabbed for his Colt.

Chapter 43

Fast as he was to react, Longarm was not nearly quick enough.

He heard Jimmy Jay's slug sizzle past his ear and strike something . . . Oh, not again, he thought.

Longarm crouched low to the ground. All the other mourners at Frankie's funeral were doing the same thing, and virtually all of the men had guns in their hands.

"Where is he? Where's the son of a bitch?"

Longarm glanced behind him. Cherie was fine. But big, beautiful Ruby was bleeding profusely from a wound at the side of her chest, close to her heart.

"He's on that knoll, beside the clump of sage," Longarm shouted, pointing. "Lay down some fire to cover me, boys. I'll go after him."

"I'm with you, mister."

"Me, too."

"He won't stick his head up to shoot again unless he wants it blown off," someone else growled.

"All right, then," Longarm said. "You men who are going with me, let's go. Ready? *Now!*"

Longarm came to his feet and charged straight at the spot where he'd seen the puff of smoke moments earlier.

Jay had chosen his ambush site unwisely this time. He was exposed out there on the prairie. Or would be.

Had he been facing only Longarm, his ambush site probably would have been fine. He would have been able to lie there taking aimed shots at an unprotected enemy for as long as he wished. But with seven other men whipping the air around him and spraying gravel into his face, Jay would not be able to stir without having a bullet put a new part in his hair.

Longarm's long legs carried him out in front of the other two, so that he was a good ten yards to the fore when he approached the concealed rifleman's shooting post.

As Longarm and the other men came near, the gunfire from Frankie's gravesite subsided, lest it hit them by accident.

Jimmy Jay rose to his knees then, exposing his upper body. He held a lever-action Winchester in his hands, a plain saddle gun with no fancy telescope sight on it.

"Drop it," Longarm warned, sliding to a stop and withholding his fire in case Jay wanted to surrender.

"Fuck you, Long." Jimmy Jay, the feared assassin who did his murdering from long range, snapped the Winchester to his shoulder.

Longarm's Colt roared and a dark red spot no larger than a silver dime appeared on the front of Jimmy Jay's shirt.

The killer blanched and seemed to lose all interest in the rifle he was holding. He looked down in apparent disbelief at the place where he'd been shot. The Winchester tumbled from his hands.

"Damn you. Damn you."

The two other men stumbled to a halt beside Longarm, both of them gasping for breath.

"You've killed me, Long."

"Yes, Jimmy, I expect that I have."

"At least that bitch is dead," Jay hissed, his breathing as labored now as that of the men who'd just sprinted the hundred yards to him.

"What are you talking about, Jimmy?"

"That red-headed bitch. She . . . she ruined my girl. Made her do . . . do terrible things. Unnatural, don't you see. Made her . . . oh, Jesus. She killed herself, Long. When that bitch from the jail was done with her. She killed herself. I had to . . . had to get even. And I did. Missed my chance at you. But I got her. I killed her, Long. Didn't I?"

"Yes, Jimmy, I expect that you did."

"And now you've killed me."

"Ayuh."

"It's gonna take me . . . take me a long time . . . to die. Isn't it?"

"It could, Jimmy. I've seen men shot like you are live for days."

"Screaming from the pain, right?"

Longarm nodded. "It can get bad. But don't worry. Well get a doc to fix you up with some laudanum to keep it from hurting so bad."

"I already told you. Fuck you, Long." J. Jimmy Jay pulled out his nickel-plated belly gun and shakily tried to take aim at Longarm.

Longarm knew good and well what the killer was up to. And couldn't blame him, really. Longarm did Jay a favor and put a bullet into his brain, to put him out of his misery.

"Mister, you didn't have to do that," one of the men beside him accused. "He was shaking so bad he couldn't have hit anything."

Longarm ignored the fellow and began walking back to Cherie and the few others who remained at the gravesite now.

It looked like George Smith's helper would have to be doing some more digging now.

Deputy U.S. attorney Charles White did not look like a happy man. He addressed himself to Billy Vail, even though Longarm was right there in the office with the two of them.

"Your man had no authority to release that prisoner. Why, she was more than a prisoner. She was our star witness. All we had on this Batson character is her word and that of Powell. Now Powell is dead and there is no telling where Cherie Johnson is. Or what she may be calling herself now. Your man fouled up this time, Vail. He has ruined our whole case."

"Bullshit, Charles," Billy Vail retorted. "You have the Mail Bomber behind bars. That will make everyone happy back east, and that is what this whole thing was really about, anyway. As for your witness, Longarm tells me she suffered two great losses in the span of a few day's time. She wanted to go home. Wherever the hell 'home' is. He did not have the heart to stop her. You can round up all the witnesses you need to prove Batson is your bomber. It does no harm for the girl to be free."

"She was being held under my authority, Vail, not his."

"That's right," Billy agreed. "And now she isn't. Do you want her back?"

"Of course I want her back. I want her for a witness."

"Fine. Issue a warrant. Wanted. One small woman. Name unknown. Whereabouts unknown. I'll be sure to put that one in with all the other outstanding warrants my people are expected to serve when they aren't out actually solving crimes or arresting dangerous felons. Is that what you want, Charles?"

White turned and gave Longarm a cold look. "Never mind what I want, Vail. You wouldn't do it anyway, even if I told you what it is."

"No, I'm sure you are right, Charles. I won't fire the deputy who brought you your Mail Bomber, plus took down J. Jimmy Jay. No, won't do that at all."

The assistant U.S. attorney grumbled a little more, but that was all he was apt to do. Longarm didn't care about that, anyway. He kept seeing the glazed, empty stare in Ruby Bradbury's eyes as she lay dying in Cherie's arms. Such a waste.

And he kept seeing, too, the emptiness in Cherie's expression afterward. Poor, pitiful Cherie. She had found someone to take care of her after Frankie was killed. Now she was dead, too. There was no way Longarm intended to force Cherie to return to Denver against her will.

Cherie had been decent about it, though. Longarm knew her true name. And where her family was, where Cherie could be located now.

He just hadn't put any of that into his report, nor told Charles White about it. Didn't damn well intend to, either. White would just have to get along without her when he prosecuted Leo Batson.

Longarm sat back with his legs crossed and pulled out a cheroot, content with the knowledge that Billy Vail would protect his backside from the Charles Whites and the political hacks who infested government at all levels. Custis Long had done his best, and that was all any man could ever hope to accomplish.

Watch for

LONGARM AND THE BOYS IN THE BACK ROOM

the 313th novel in the exciting LONGARM
series from Jove

Coming in December!

LONGARM

Explore the exciting Old West with one of the men who made it wild!

J. R. ROBERTS
THE GUNSMITH